On My Own Terms

Grasy Bickett

Contents

Chapter 1

C hapter 1

"Logan Fitzgerald. Infinity Cooper. I'm coming for you."

I quickly sat up in my bed, breathing heavily. Those words had been haunting me for who knows how long. I hadn't slept for days, those words keeping me up at night.

I looked at my alarm clock, sighing at the time. 2:30am. I laid back down, rubbing my forehead as I tried pushing those words out of my mind. However, I had no luck whatsoever. It was basically a routine for me. I would fall asleep around midnight, wake up between two and three, then unable to fall asleep until at least five.

My cell phone rang quietly, so I looked at the caller id before answering. "Hello?"

"Hey, Fin," my boyfriend, Logan, said on the other line. "I figured you'd be awake. Can't sleep?"

I sighed. "No. I tried. Why is it so hard?"

"I wish I knew," Logan said. "I'm lucky to even get six hours of sleep."

"What if it's always like this?" I asked. "What if...."

"Fin, we'll get through this," Logan assured, but I heard the doubt in his voice. It was kind of hard to believe we were going to get through the situation we were in. Having the most wanted man in the country after the two of us wasn't something that I thought we could make through. "Anyway, I just wanted to call you to tell you I love you."

"I love you, too," I said.

"Try getting some sleep, okay?" he said. "I'll see you tomorrow."

"Bye," I said before hanging up and placing my cell phone back on the nightstand. Now if I could only get some sleep.

~*~

"Fin," a soft voice said. I slowly opened my eyes, trying to get them to adjust to the light. Very faintly, I saw my mom kneeling by the edge of my bed. "Time to get up for school. You're already late as it is."

I sighed, closing my eyes again. "Can't I just stay home today? Or every other day? I didn't get any sleep last night."

"I know this is hard for you, Infinity," Mom said. "But you can't let it stop you from going to school."

I opened my eyes again, looking at her with furrowed eyebrows. "Mom, some man, a very murderous man, is out to get me all because I did everything those sick people wanted. It's not my fault I can't sleep or even focus in class. I'm terrified."

"I know you are," Mom said. "I'm terrified for you. Flynn hasn't talked in weeks. We're all worried. I'll let you stay home today, but only today. I need to head off to work anyway and I can't wait for you and Flynn to get ready."

"Thanks," I said before she left my room.

It was true that a murderous man was after both me and Logan. We did nothing wrong. All we did was complete ten tasks that a group he created forced us to do. However, the founder of the group didn't seem to like that. Now, he escaped prison and announced on a broadcast that he was coming for us.

Oddly enough, my fourteen year old brother is the one affected the most. Ever since the broadcast, he hasn't uttered a single word, which is odd for him since he was not only a talkative one, but a joker. I really missed his jokes.

I texted Logan and my best friend, Lilly, telling them that I wouldn't be at school. The last thing I need was for them to worry.

After laying back down on my bed, my brother walked in my room, his hair all over the place and a blanket wrapped around him. He sat down at the foot of my bed, reaching for the TV remote and turning it on. I was used to this. He always came in my room and either slept on the ground, or watched TV. I hated seeing my brother so depressed.

Shortly after I heard my mom leave, I heard the front door open followed by footsteps coming up the stairs. Logan appeared in the doorway. "Are you okay?" he asked. "I brought some chicken noodle soup and chocolate and...."

I sat up. "Logan, I'm fine," I interrupted. "I'm just tried so I asked my mom if I could stay home. But thanks."

Logan sat down beside me, placing a grocery bag on the nightstand. "Sorry. I got worried when you sent me the text."

"Logan, don't worry," I said. "You're worried, that's normal. Then again, what do I know about normal?"

Logan wrapped his arm around me. "It's okay, Fin," he said softly. "How's your brother?"

I gestured my chin towards Flynn, whose eyes was glued on the TV. "The same," I said. "I really miss the jokes he had."

"He's just in shock," Logan said.

"For weeks?" I asked.

"Maybe because he's afraid of losing his sister," Logan said. "He already lost his parents."

"I know," I said as I dug through the grocery bag. Logan brought a lot of chocolate bars. He was the sweetest boyfriend ever. I pulled out a KitKat bar and handed it to Flynn, who accepted it without saying a word. There had to be something I could do to get him talking again.

I scooted forward on the bed, sitting beside Flynn. Logan did the same and sat on the other side. "Things would be easier if you would talk," I said to him.

Flynn looked down at the chocolate bar in his hands, still not uttering a single word.

"Flynn, I know you're scared," I said. "All of us are. But hiding away in this little shell of yours isn't healthy. You need to be yourself again."

"You don't get it," Flynn said quietly. Even though the words were sad, I almost smiled at hearing his voice again. "I didn't get to see my parents at the time of their death. I got called down to the office at school where they told me that they died in a car crash. And now, my sister is being hunted by a crazy mad man because he's a hypocrite. I can't lose my older sister."

I pulled Flynn into a hug. "Flynn, I promise you won't lose me." I was doubtful of it, but I had to convince him otherwise.

"We're not going to give up," Logan said. "We're not going down without a fight. The cops are doing the best they can to find him. They're keeping a close eye on our houses. Nobody is letting us go through this alone."

"That man broke out of jail," Flynn pointed out. "You think he won't be able to get pass a few cops? They haven't been able to track him down yet. He won't be found."

"Flynn...."

"I'm going to eat," he muttered before getting off the bed and heading out of my room.

I sighed, hating the way he was feeling. We were all worried, but he was the one who was letting it affect him the most.

"Wow," Logan said. "Even my siblings aren't acting like that."

"Do you think he's right?" I asked. "The cops haven't tracked him down yet and he was able to break out of jail."

I shrugged. "I don't know. We just have to hope for the best."

Chapter 2

C hapter 2

"Infinity!" Mom called from the kitchen. "Can you come here please?!"

I sighed, pulling myself up from the couch and walking to the kitchen. Mom was running back and forth from the stove and one of the counters. "Yes?"

"Would you be able to run to the store and get some chocolate cheesecake?" she asked without even looking at me. She was way too busy making dinner.

"Mom, there's no point," I said. "He's still not going to talk." Lately, Mom has been making or buying all of Flynn's favorite foods in an attempt to get him to talk again and be himself. He did talk to me and Logan the day before, but that was it. And it was only for him to tell us why he was so upset.

"Please?" Mom asked. "I know it won't change anything, but I need to show Flynn that we are here for him."

"So spoiling him with his favorite foods will show him that we're here for him?" I asked. "Mom, Logan and I both tried talking to him. Jake tried talking to him. Nothing is working."

Mom sighed. "I know that. I want to see him smile. I know how much he loves chocolate cheese cake. I'm hoping he'll smile when he sees it for dessert."

"Fine," I said. I really wanted to see Flynn smile again as well, so I had to agree. "I'll go." I walked out of the kitchen and went to the living room. Logan was sitting on the couch where I left him. We were at each other's house almost all the time. I felt safer with him near me. "Logan, can you take me to the grocery store? My mom wants me to get some chocolate cheesecake."

"Sure," he said, standing up from the couch and putting his cell phone in the pocket of his jeans. He led me outside of my house after Mom gave me some money, and to his car. I climbed in the passenger seat and immediately sighed. "You okay, Fin?"

"Of course not," I said as he started up his car. "Don't you ever miss Flynn's random jokes or when he makes no sense?"

"All the time," Logan said. "That guy always had something that a smart-aleck would say. Even though it got annoying, I miss it. You and your mom tried doing everything?"

I nodded. "Yup. Getting his favorite foods, watching his favorite movies, trying to talk to him. Nothing works. Do you have any ideas?"

"I wish," Logan said. "Trust me, if I had any ideas, I would try."

The rest of the ride to the grocery store was quiet, and thankfully it wasn't too far. When we got there, Logan and I went to the dessert aisle. After picking up the cheesecake, we walked through other aisles to see if there were any snacks we could get, even though Mom was making dinner.

I stopped when I saw a large bottle of soda. I softly chuckled. "Remember that time when Flynn decided to spray us with soda because apparently, we were being too lovey-dovey."

Logan chuckled as well. "How could I forget? My hair was sticky for the longest time."

I grabbed the bottle of soda, telling Logan it was the flavor Flynn liked. I knew I told my mom that buying my brother's favorite food wouldn't help him, but there was nothing else to do.

We went out to the checkout, paying for the two items. The cashier, a girl who went to our school, seemed a bit nervous to check out our items. Ever since everyone in our town found out that Logan and I were targeted by Ryan Sage, one of the most violet men in the world. He created a group, Death by Death, and they targeted innocent people, forcing them to do tasks. And the only way to survive was to complete all ten tasks.

Nobody has ever completed them before except for me and Logan.

Everyone was also so nervous around us. Most of the time, I hated it. But other times, I was thankful that girls, especially the cheerleaders, no longer flirted with Logan when they knew he had a girlfriend.

We paid for the items and went back to Logan's car. When we got to my house, I set the cake and soda on the counter. Dinner was made and both Mom and Flynn were sitting at the table. Logan and I sat down in the two empty seats and began eating the bowl of spaghetti, once of Flynn's favorite meals. However, he still looked the same; sad and lost in space.

"Fin and Logan got dessert," Mom said to Flynn. "Chocolate cheesecake."

Flynn didn't reply as he repeatedly spun his spaghetti on his fork, not even eating it. I sighed, getting up from my seat and pouring four small glasses of the soda. I sat them down in front of everyone, getting a thank you from both Logan and Mom. Like always, Flynn said nothing.

After a very quiet dinner, Mom served the dessert. Flynn, who didn't even finish the spaghetti, accepted the cake and stabbed it repeatedly with his fork.

Mom finished her cake and announced that she was going to be in her office for the rest of the night. Logan helped me clean up the kitchen as Flynn stayed where he was. I hated seeing my little brother like this.

Logan and I walked out of the kitchen, leaving Flynn in the kitchen. "Do you think he's going to stay like this forever?" I asked Logan once we were standing in the living room.

"I really don't know, Fin," Logan said. "I know it hurts for you to see him like this. It hurts me to and he's not even my brother." He gently intertwined his hands with mine and held them between us. "We'll get through this. It seems tough, but we just have to stick together."

I gave him a faint smile. "Yeah. Together."

He removed one of his hands from mine and brushed a few strands of hair out of my face. "Fin, don't worry about it," he said. "I know this isn't just about Flynn. You're also worried about Ryan finding us. What's the worst he can do? He's just a man."

"One who has been in prison and broke out," I said. "And the man who created the most dangerous group in the country. Innocent people died because of him, Logan."

"This is about your dad, isn't it?" Logan asked. I nodded. "I'm sorry about him, you know. I wish you got to know him."

"Yeah, me too," I said quietly, looking down. My dad was a victim of Death by Death while my mom was pregnant with me. He got into a car crash while doing one of the tasks and didn't survive. I never even got to meet him.

Logan gently placed his thumb under my chin and lifted it up to face me. "Hey. You still have your mom and brother and Lilly and me. We're all here for you, especially me. I'll always be here for you." He lowered his head and pressed his lips onto mine.

Suddenly, Logan and I both got soaked with a sticky liquid. We pulled away and I saw Flynn holding the bottle of soda, a wide smile on his face. "No lovey-dovey stuff," he said.

"Flynn!" I said, trying to wipe the soda off of me. However, it was already sticking onto my skin.

"Oh, I'm sorry," he said. "The soda slipped from my hand."

"Really?" I asked. "The soda slipped?"

"Yup," he said. "Oh, and by the way....I'm back."

____

Flynn is back to himself. (: He's a little mischievous at times, though, so expect many not-so-harmless pranks.

Chapter 3

C hapter 3

I had always hated going to school. I wasn't really that popular with people and this one girl was particularly such a bully. Then Logan moved back here. We moved away when he was twelve and he was my and Lilly's close friend. So when he came back, he immediately hung out with us. A lot of girls didn't like it because he was, apparently, voted the hottest guy in school. I hated it. There shouldn't be a hottest guy or girl because looks didn't matter.

But ever since that broadcast, I hated going even more. People kept staring at my, looking quite terrified. At least I still had Lilly and Logan by my side.

When lunch rolled around, I sat down at the table Lilly, Logan, and I normally sat at. I was the first one there since my class was closest to the cafeteria. Everyone one else made sure they sat far away from me.

Lilly sat down across from me as a pair of arms gently wrapped around me. "How are you?" Logan asked softly.

"Tired," I replied. "At least Flynn is back to normal."

Logan kissed the side of my head before sitting down beside me. "Yeah, that's good," Logan said. "I mean, I hate getting soaked in soda, but at least it means he's not shutting anyone out again."

"Did he really spray the both of you with soda?" Lilly asked with a raised eyebrow.

"Yes," I said with a scowl. "Just because we were being to lovey-dovey." I rolled my eyes. Logan and I weren't that lovey-dovey.

Lilly, however, smiled at that. "You know, I should have bet on you to finally ending up together. I would have been rich!"

Logan chuckled a bit at this. Ever since we were ten, Lilly kept saying that I was going to marry Logan in the future, even though I denied it a few times. Then when he came back here, I shortly realized I had feelings for him. He knew everything about me and he was always there for me. He was one of my best friends.

"I told you, Fin," Lilly said. "I knew the whole time you liked him, even if you denied it."

"I was ten," I pointed out.

"You're never to young for a crush," Lilly said. "I remember when I was seven and I had a crush on this boy. He shared his box of crayons with me, but then I saw him on the swings with another girl. It broke my little heart."

I rolled my eyes. Lilly was always so hyper and crazy. But it was what I liked about her.

"But anyway, I'm happy my OTP is still staying strong," she said. "But," she pointed her fork at Logan, "if you ever hurt her like Toby did, you will see my wrath. And you do not want to see my wrath. Got it?!"

I looked at her with a raised eyebrow. "How much cups of coffee did you have this morning?" I asked. She was a lot more hyper than usual.

"Only three, I swear," she said. "I didn't get any sleep last night because I was reading about Ryan and then I decided to watch a movie with a really hot guy in it and then I had to stalk that guy on all his social media sites and then I got hungry and I ate some candy because it was the closest thing to me and I did not want to get out of bed."

"How fun," Logan said sarcastically as he began eating his lunch.

I wasn't that hungry, so I basically just peeled the crust off my sandwich and took small bites. Logan was looking at me with a concerned look, but I assured him that I was feeling alright.

I basically ate only half of my sandwich before decided that I couldn't eat anymore. I haven't had an appetite in such a long time.

When the bell rang to end lunch, Logan took my hand in his and helped me up. He grabbed all the garbage with his free hand and threw it in a nearby garbage. Then, the three of us had to head to one of the classes I couldn't stand; gym. My teacher, Mr. Wilkie, sort of had an obsession with dodgeball and we were playing it constantly. It was getting annoying, especially because I sucked at the game.

While we were walking to the gym, Logan wrapped his arm around my shoulder, pulling my into him. My arms went around his waist, feeling comfortable in his embrace. Just by hugging him, I felt a lot better.

"Are you okay?" he asked softly.

I nodded. "Yeah, I guess. I'm still feeling the same, so there's not really a change."

"We'll get through this," he assured. "I know it's hard, but we will."

"Hopefully," I said. It just seemed so hard that we would be able to get through this. It seemed easy; all that had to be done was the police capturing Ryan. It was only him that was after us.

When we got to the gym, we had about five minutes after the late bell to get changed. However, I was already wearing sweats so I didn't have to. Logan as well, so we sat down on one of the bleachers.

"I'm not going to lie," Logan said, intertwining his hand with mine and squeezing it lightly. "I've been freaking out everyday about Ryan and the whole Death by Death thing. I'm worried that Ryan will be able to find us before the police find him. And I'm worried you'll get hurt, or even worse than that."

"You don't seem like you're freaking out," I muttered.

"Well, I am," he said. "I have nightmares. I have nightmares where he finds you and he...." He sighed and shook his head, running his free hand through his brown hair. "I guess I hide it really well." He angle himself so he faced me better, taking my other hands in his. "Fin, if it comes between you and me, I'm going to do everything to make sure you survive. Even if it means that I won't."

"Logan, don't say that," I said. "We're both going to survive, okay?"

"Do you really think that?" he asked.

I didn't answer because if I was honest, I wasn't so sure.

Sorry for the long wait between the updates. cx I had a writer's block because I didn't really plan this out that well. I'm sort of writing it as I go. I have the ending planned out, that's about it. cx

I'll try my best to upload once a week though, possibly every Monday.

Chapter 4

Chapter 4

I heard someone walk in my room, but I ignored it. I was still very tired and not in the mood to wake up. I was hoping whoever walked in my room would go away and leave me to sleep, but that was not the case.

"Fin!" I heard my younger brother yell as someone jumped on my bed. "Fin! Wake up! You have to wake up!"

I groaned and opened my eyes, seeing my younger brother grinning deviously at me. "What the hell, Flynn?" I asked.

"Whoa, watch your language," Flynn said. "Come on, you have to get out of bed!"

"It's Saturday," I whined. "Why do I have to get out of bed?"

"It's Logan."

I sat up straight and looked at Flynn. "What about Logan? Is he okay?"

Flynn shrugged. "I don't know. He's probably still sleeping right now. I just wanted you to get up."

I glared at him and smacked him in the face with my pillow. "Screw off, Flynn," I said. "That was not funny. I thought something bad happened."

"I just wanted you to get up," he said innocently. "I'm bored." He flopped down on the bottom half of my bed with a pouty look. "Can we play Minecraft?"

"I'm still tired," I said. "Why don't you go to Jake's house?"

"Because it's so far," he whined. "I have to walk for, like, twenty minutes and then I'll have to walk back. Please can we play Minecraft?"

"You can play it by yourself," I said as I laid back down. "I'm going back to bed."

I felt Flynn get off my bed and I thought he was actually going to let me sleep in. However, it wasn't long before he came back in my room and did something I never thought he would do while I was in bed.

He literally dumped a whole can of soda on me.

I sat up quickly, wiping the sticky liquid from my face. "What the hell is your problem, Flynn? I'm trying to sleep!"

He gave me a smile. "You can't now. It will be too hard, so you can play Minecraft with me."

"No," I said. "Now, I have to throw my bedding in the washer machine and have a shower. So, good job, Flynn. Your plan backfired."

Flynn groaned dramatically and stormed out of my room. "Thank you for being a wonderful sister and not playing games with me!" he called sarcastically as he walked away.

I sighed, pulling myself out of bed and taking off my bedding. I carried it downstairs and went to the laundry room. As much as I loved having

Flynn back to himself, I hated when he acted like this. He would never let me sleep in, he was always pouring soda on me, and he was constantly complaining about me not playing games with him, even though I did a lot.

After I put my bedding in the wash, I went to the washroom to have a quick shower. I scoffed when I walked in, seeing a mess of Flynn's stuff. Before he was adopted, both my mom and I had our own washroom since there was two, but now I had to share with him. And it was annoying. He was so messy, constantly leaving his clothes on the floor even though the laundry basket was close by.

I took a quick shower, washing the soda off of me. I had to do this at least once a week because Flynn had a serious problem with dumping soda on people.

When I finished my shower, I changed into some comfortable clothes right before I heard the doorbell ring. "FIN!" Flynn called from his bedroom. "ANSWER THE DOOR!"

I sighed, walking out of my room. "You do know I'm older than you, right?!" I called back. "I don't have to listen to you!"

He didn't reply as I walked down the stairs and answered the door. Logan was standing there with his younger brother, Jake. Jake was Flynn's age and they were the best of friends. "Hi," Logan said. "Flynn wanted Jake to come over, so I thought I'd come as well."

I let them in and closed the door behind them. "Jake!" Flynn exclaimed as he hurried down the stairs.

"Flynn!" Jake exclaimed back. They then did this really weird hug that nobody quite understood.

"Well, the bromance game is strong," Logan commented.

"And awesome," Flynn said. "Dude, let's play Minecraft!"

"Yes!" Jake said before he and Flynn rushed upstairs.

"I'll never understand them," I said.

"Same," Logan said. He reached up and gently tugged on a strand of my hair since it was still damp from the shower. "Let me guess. Soda?"

I scoffed. "While I was trying to sleep. So now my bedding is in the wash."

Logan chuckled. "I have no idea what's up with your brother and soda."

"At least he's back to himself," I said. "Want to watch a movie? I can make some popcorn, salt and vinegar flavor, your favorite."

Logan smiled. "Sure. Want me to pick to movie while and you make the popcorn?"

I nodded before I went to the kitchen as he headed to the living room. I first popped the popcorn before adding the butter and Logan's favorite flavoring. When it had the perfect amount of flavoring, I went into the living room with the large bowl and sat down beside Logan. I rested the bowl on my leg and his leg as he started the movie.

I rested my head on Logan's shoulder, feeling comfortable sitting beside him. For a long time, I was always worrying about Ryan and whether or not he would get to us before the police found him. However, every time I was with Logan, it made me feel better and safe.

"I like this movie," I said about five minutes into it. It was one that Logan and I had seen many times before. It never got old.

"Yeah," Logan agreed. "The only part that I don't get is the ending. I like the ending, I just don't get it."

"Same here," I said, taking a handful of popcorn and basically shoving it in my face.

"Ooh, popcorn!" I heard Flynn say. "Can we have some?!"

I turned to face him, seeing both him and Jake with eager expressions as they stared t the popcorn. "Uh, no," I said. "And what happened to Minecraft?"

"We smelled the popcorn," Flynn said. "Be wonderful siblings and share."

"You have your own hands, go make your own," I said.

Flynn frowned, then smiled deviously. "If you don't share, I'll spray soda on you."

"If you spray soda on us, I'll continuously kiss your sister whenever you're around," Logan said, knowing it bothered Flynn whenever Logan and I kissed.

Flynn pretended to gag. "Never mind, I'll go make my own popcorn. Come on, Jake. Let's go make popcorn that's better than theirs." They headed off into the kitchen.

"Well, that worked," Logan said. "But I'm going to kiss you anyway." He pressed his lips softly on mine before turning back to the movie. "I love you, Fin," he said.

"I love you too, Logan," I replied, snuggling into him. I loved spending time with him, but I was worried our time together may be limited. If the police couldn't capture Ryan, we wouldn't be guaranteed to survive. He was a deadly man and I had no idea what he was capable of. But seeing as he broke out of prison, he could probably do a whole lot.

Including killing the two teenagers he was after. Logan and I were going to have to find a way to get out of this before Ryan found us. If only it seemed possible.

————————

So I will be updating every Monday now for sure. I'm rarely busy Monday's so I have a lot of time to work on the parts.

I seriously love Flynn and Jake's bromance. cx They're definitely the best of friends.

Chapter 5

C hapter 5

I hated not being able to sleep. I was always so tired at nights, but nothing could make me fall asleep. I tossed and turned in bed, trying to get even one hour of sleep, but it was no use. Those words were still stuck in my head and I couldn't get them out. Logan Fitzgerald. Infinity Cooper. I'm coming for you.

I finally couldn't take it anymore and pulled myself out of bed, looking at the clock on my nightstand. One in the morning. Not too early to go for a walk, right?

I grabbed one of Logan's old hoodies that he gave me -though it was more like me taking it without him knowing- and pulled it over my head before I went downstairs. I slowly opened the front door, hoping I wouldn't wake my mom or my brother.

"Fin?" a quiet voice suddenly asked. I turned to the stairs, seeing Flynn standing at the top. He was standing there with a blanket wrapped tightly around him. His blond hair was sticking up all over the place and he looked like he never got any sleep yet either. "Where are you going?"

"For a walk," I replied.

Flynn frowned. "At one in the morning? Isn't that dangerous?"

"No," I said. "Besides, Ryan isn't in this state." I didn't know when he would arrive in Vermont, and that was what was bothering me.

"But...." he began to object, but I didn't let him finish.

"I'll be fine, Flynn," I said. "I promise."

"Can't you just walk around in the backyard?" he asked. He was really worried about me.

"I promise I'll be fine," I repeated. "There's nothing to worry about, okay? Just go back to bed."

Flynn stared at me for a bit before sighing and going back to his bedroom. Sometimes, I forgot he was a fourteen year old boy. Most fourteen year olds wouldn't be worrying about their seventeen year old sister if she wanted to go for a walk.

Making sure I had my cell phone and house keys, I walked out of the house and locked the door behind me. Only a few cars were passing by, so it was really peaceful outside. I took a deep breath of the fresh air before shoving my hands in the pocket of my hoodie before starting my walk.

Maybe I should have done this more often. It felt nice to walk around in the dark, even though it was one in the morning. The only thing dangerous about this town was Death by Death, so I was even feeling a bit safe walking around.

Within five minutes of my walk, my cell phone began to rang. I quickly answered it, seeing Logan's name as the caller id. "Hello?"

"Fin," he said, his voice cracking a bit.

"Logan, what's wrong?" I asked. "Are you okay?"

"He's....He was last spotted in New York," Logan said.

"New York?" I asked. "That's...."

"Right beside our state," Logan finished. "He was spotted in Syracuse, which is far from here, but not that far. By driving, it's five hours away. He can be here by six o'clock."

My heart started beating faster. "How could he get there that fast? He was in California. That's....that's all the way across the country."

"I don't know," Logan said. "He's one of the most dangerous people in America. Of course he can get around that fast."

"We....we can die in a few hours. He's going to kill us."

"We don't know that for sure," Logan said.

"He said he's coming for us," I said. "What else will he do?"

Logan sighed. "I don't know, Fin. But the police was already informed about Ryan being close to here. There's at least two people, some not even cops, stationed at each entrance of our town. A lot of people want him caught."

"He made it through a lot of states without getting caught," I said. "I'm pretty sure he can get in without getting caught. And what happens when he does? What happens when he finds us? What happens when...."

"Infinity," Logan interrupted. "Stop worrying, alright? The cops are going to try their best to catch Ryan. Everyone wants to see him locked up again and when, not if, when he gets arrested again, he'll be under a better surveillance now that they know he can escape. But worrying about it, filling your mind with negative outcomes, won't help."

I sighed. "I can't help it, Logan. I'm scared."

"I know," Logan said. "I am too, trust me. But I can't worry about it. I have to show everyone, especially you, that I'm not letting this effect me."

"It's hard for me," I said. "You know it is. I saw my best friend die for me and then it turned out she was alive, all because of this stupid Death by Death thing. My dad died because of it. What if we're next, Logan? My brother will lose someone else he cares about. My mom will lose yet another family member because of Death by Death. It's ruining my life."

"Fin," Logan said, but it wasn't just over the phone. I turned around to see him standing behind me, his cell phone held up to his ear. "What are you doing out here?"

I hung up and put my phone back into my pocket. "I needed to go for a walk. What about you?"

"I was heading to your house," Logan said. He then held out his arms. "Come here."

As soon as he said that, I wrapped my arms tightly around him, digging my face into his chest as I let the tears escape. I just wanted all of this to be over. I didn't want to live in fear any longer. It was hurting me. It was hurting my family and friends. We were all living in fear, wondering when Ryan would come and attack.

"It's okay," Logan said softly. "We'll be fine."

"You don't know that," I muttered into his chest.

Logan sighed. "I know. I'm just trying to be positive."

I looked up at him and he wiped my tears away. "I can't. I'm trying, but I can't. It's hard."

"I know," Logan said. "Come on, let's go to your house."

He wrapped his arm around my shoulder and led me back to my house. My hands were too shaky to unlock the door, so he did it for me. After walking inside, he locked the door behind him before taking my hand in his and leading me to my room.

Logan was about to take a blanket and pillow off my bed to sleep on the floor, but I stopped him. "Can you lay down with me?" I asked quietly.

"Yeah, of course," Logan said.

We both got onto my bed and I rested my head on his chest, hoping his heart beat would be soothing enough to help me fall asleep. It was.

———————————

I'm so sorry for the long wait for an update. However, I kind of have an idea where this story is going now, so there might be an update once a week. There might be.

Chapter 6

C hapter 6

The lights flickering on and off was what woke me up, unfortunately. I was actually able to fall asleep without anything from Death by Death haunting me. Maybe all I needed was to be close to Logan.

I slowly opened my eyes and looked tiredly at the door. Logan was awake too, but he kept his eyes closed as he stirred a bit.

Flynn was standing by the door, his hand resting on the light switch. "Flynn, why did you wake us?" I whined.

"Because I'm awake and Mom's at work, and I don't want to be the only one awake," Flynn said. "Why is Logan here? Did you two do the frickle frackles last night?"

I glared at Flynn and threw one of my pillows at him. "Must you be so annoying?" I asked.

"Yup," Flynn said smugly before hopping onto my bed, the movement making Logan groan and put his arm over his eyes. "Come on, Logan-bear. Get up."

"I'd rather stay asleep forever," Logan said. "And escape reality."

I sighed and laid back down, my head resting on Logan's chest. "Flynn, Ryan was spotted in Syracuse around one in the morning," I said.

Flynn frowned. "That's about how far? Five hours away?"

"Yeah," I said. "He can be in this town any minute, even though there are people by every entrance."

"But that was at one in the morning," Flynn said. "That was ten hours ago."

I furrowed my eyebrows. "It's eleven?"

"Yeah," Flynn said. "So, it's either he's here and nobody spotted him, or he's hiding in a different city because he knows he's expected here."

"Logan, what if this is it?" I asked. "What if he's here and finds us today?"

Logan removed his arm from over his eyes and looked at me. "Fin, don't say that. Look, I was thinking about what Ryan said and how he's coming after us. He didn't technically say anything about killing us."

"But he's the founder of a group that gave people tasks, otherwise they would be killed," I pointed out. "Their name is Death by Death. Killing people, as sick as it is, is their thing."

Logan sat up, making me sit up with him. He wrapped his arm around me and rested his chin on my head, not saying anything else. He probably realized that I was right.

"I have a theory," Flynn spoke up. "I really don't think Ryan will kill you on the spot or anything like that. He was in prison and if he gets caught again, he'll be in prison even longer with even stricter guards, especially if he purposefully killed two teenagers for no reason."

"Then why else would he be after us?" I asked. "What else is there for him to do?"

Flynn sighed. "That, I don't know. But it should give you some hope, right?"

"I hate to admit it, Flynn, but my hope is long gone," I said. "I'm only seventeen years old and I'm scared for my life. I can't help thinking that's there's nothing we can do."

"Fin, listen to me," Logan said. "That was what we thought when we were on Death Watch, right? We thought there was nothing we could do, but get this. We pulled our way through and finished all ten tasks. We can pull our way through this."

Logan did have a point but for some reason, I couldn't convince myself at that. Having to complete those tasks were worse than having one man after us, but it didn't feel that way.

Logan got up from the bed and pulled me up us well. Without saying a word, he held my hand and led me downstairs to my kitchen. He opened the freezer, which caused me to immediately furrow my eyebrows. "What are you doing?" I asked.

"Doing what we usually do when I want to cheer you up," he replied, taking my mint chocolate chip ice cream container out of the fridge. "We are going to be making a sundae."

"Logan, I'm not in the mood for sundaes," I said.

"Which is what you say every single time I suggest making sundaes," Logan said, placing the container on the counter before going to the fridge. "And you still eat it and feel better afterwards."

"Logan...."

Logan continued ignoring my objections as he pulled out all kinds of ingredients; whipped cream, cherries, strawberries, chocolate sauce, caramel sauce....He then went to the snack cupboard and pulled out a bar of Kit Kat, one of my weaknesses.

"Alright, fine," I said, standing beside him as he placed a bowl on the counter. "We'll make the stupid sundae."

Logan gave me a smile before scooping some of the ice cream in the bowl. He added all of my favorite ingredients before topping it off with whipped cream. "This enough?" he asked.

I looked at the whipped cream in the bowl. "More," I said. Logan added a bit more, then stopped. "More." He raised an eyebrow and added more. "Hmm....More."

Logan rolled his eyes before adding even more. "There, is that enough?"

"No," I said. "More."

Logan then sprayed some of the whipped cream on my nose. "There."

"Logan!" I exclaimed, though there was a smile on my face. "You'll pay for that!"

I tried grabbing the whipped cream bottle from him, but he held it out of my grasp since he was taller than me, and he only sprayed me some more. At one part, I was able to push the nozzle and get some on him.

We ended up wasting all the whipped cream and we had a lot of it on our faces. I couldn't help but smile as I reached up and pulled Logan to my level, pressing my whipped cream covered lips against his. For a moment, I was feeling like I used to before we got involved with Death by Death. For a moment, I felt safe.

When we pulled away from each other, we cleaned up with paper towels before bringing the ice cream sundae to the dining room table to eat. Right as we finished, I got a call from my mom. She told me she was working overtime today and needed me and Flynn to go to the store to pick up some things for dinner.

I told Logan and he offered to clean up while I got ready to leave, since I was still in my pajamas. I told Flynn we had to go to the store before getting ready.

When we were both ready to go, we went downstairs where Logan was waiting by the front door. I went to the cookie jar we used to keep money inside just in case and grabbed two twenties. Mom texted me the list and it didn't look like it would cost more than forty dollars.

Since Logan's car was still at his house, we walked to the grocery store. I knew as soon as we were to get there, Flynn would beg me for a chocolate bar.

He did. And not wanting to hear him complain, I told him to go pick out a chocolate bar, because I knew how long that would take him, while Logan and I got the groceries.

By the time Logan and I were finished, Flynn was still deciding what chocolate bar to get. He was stuck between two choices, so I told him to just get one of each. Although, that could have been his plan so he would get two....

After we finished paying, we began walking back to the house. However, I couldn't help but feel something ominous. I quickly looked behind us, but I didn't see anything out of the ordinary.

While we were walking by an alley, the ominous feeling was confirmed when a man stepped out and right in front of us. But not just any man. A man I had seen on the news, online, anywhere except for real life.

Ryan Sage.

He was able to get into our town without being spotted.

My heart began beating faster, especially by seeing his cruel smirk. "Well, well, well. If it isn't Logan Fitzgerald and Infinity Cooper. Oh, and I see little Flynn Cooper here as well. Such a cute scene. I bet you've been expecting me."

Neither of us replied. We couldn't. I couldn't. I was terrified of this guy. He caused nightmares for me and Logan, no matter how brave Logan seemed. He caused Flynn to be so....un-Flynn-like for weeks.

"So, here's what's going to happen," Ryan said. "I'm not going to kill you."

Wait. What?

"Since you two decided to cheat your way out of the ten tasks, I'm assigning you another ten," he said. "But these ten....Oh, these ten are going to be very impossible to do. In fact, some, if not all, you might not even make it through alive."

"What if we do?" Logan asked, his voice strained.

Ryan chuckled. "You won't."

"What if we do?" Logan asked again.

"If?" Ryan repeated. "There is no if. But I'll humor you. If you two so happen to make it through, without cheating your way out, I'll let you go. But there are some obligations. You do not tell the police, or anyone for that matter, that I am here and have given you more tasks, not even your family."

"Deal," Logan said. We didn't really have a choice.

"Oh, and there's one more thing," Ryan said. "It won't be just you two doing the tasks. I think little Flynn is going to join you two as well. The more the merrier."

I looked over at Flynn, who was staring at Ryan in shock. My little brother was going to be doing the tasks with us? No, that wasn't fair!

"That's not fair!" I found myself saying. "He wasn't even on Death Watch!"

"Aww, that sucks," Ryan said. "It's all three of you, or I will actually kill you. Got it?"

"Yeah," Flynn said quietly. "Got it."

"Good," Ryan said. "I'll give you more information on your task soon. Until then, have a very good day." We watched as Ryan disappeared into the alley.

When he told me and Logan that we had to do more tasks, I thought it was the end of the line. But then Ryan added my brother into the mix. And since he did that, one thing is for sure.

We were going to survive. I was not going to let Ryan win.

I was going to survive on my own terms.

———————————

That title reference at the end, though. cx

I am sorry for the two months between the updates. I don't know why I couldn't write this chapter. I knew that I wanted to write, but I, for some reason, didn't have the motivation.

There will still be slow updates, but I think I know where this story is going now, so I'll try to update at least once per week, if not, every two weeks. That's fair, right? cx

And if I didn't update in two weeks, feel free to spam me with messages so I'll write. cx

Chapter 7

C hapter 7

On Sunday morning, I pulled myself out of bed to eat. I got n sleep last night. Well, I might have slept for an hour, but that was about it. My mind was too occupied thinking about the new tasks we had to do. Ryan said they were going to be next to impossible and there was a low chance of us surviving.

However, as much as my hope was gone, my determination wasn't. Ryan made the wrong move by involving my little brother in this. We were going to survive.

I walked in the kitchen, noticing a small package sitting on the table. Beside it was a note from my mom, telling me that this was sitting on the front steps for me when she was about to leave for work. I picked up the package, noticing a piece of paper taped to it. I gently took it off and read it.

My dearest Infinity. This will be used for me to contact you. I don't trust sending the tasks on your own cell phone. Be prepared to receive your first task some time today. -Yours truly....Well, you know.

Hesitantly, I opened the package, only to see a cell phone sitting on the bottom. This guys was being extremely cautious.

"What's that?" I heard Flynn ask me.

I turned to face him and took the cell phone out of the package. "Communication," I said before noticing how Flynn looked. His hair was sticking up all over the place and he had huge bags under his eyes. Not to mention he had his blanket wrapped around him tightly. "No sleep?"

Flynn shook his head and yawned. "I was up all night thinking about possible tasks. I thought the last ones were hard and I only did one of them with you. One that sent me to the hospital....Anyway, I thought up of all different tasks, which is only freaking me out more."

"Well, we should be getting one sometime today," I said. "I know he said it will be impossible, but I'm really wishing the first one starts off easy."

Flynn snorted. "Yeah, right. I bet you anything it's going to start off hard."

"I wouldn't doubt it," I said with a sigh. "I'm going to call Logan." I went up to my bedroom to get my cell phone. It was still quite early, but I knew that Logan would either wake up immediately to me calling, or he was already awake because he didn't get enough sleep last night.

I was right. He answered right away, not even letting the cell phone ring a full time. "Fin, is everything okay?" he asked in a worried tone.

That, however, made me smile. "You're cute when you worry."

"So nothing's wrong?" he asked.

"Not really," I said. "I got a package from Ryan. A cell phone, to be exact. We're using it for communication and we should be getting the first task today."

"Oh," he said. "Okay, I'll be on my way."

"You know you don't have to come over, right?" I asked. "I just wanted to tell you."

"I'm still coming over," Logan said. "Just to hang out, I guess."

I furrowed my eyebrows. "You guess? Logan, is everything okay with you?"

Logan sighed. "No, Fin, it's not. I....I'll tell you when I get there."

"Okay," I said. "I guess I'll see you soon. I love you, Logan."

"I love you too, Infinity," he said before hanging up. Something was definitely wrong with him. Even throughout this situation, he wasn't too upset but with our just-then conversation, he seemed way too upset.

I got changed before heading back down the stairs where Flynn was stuffing his face with chips while he watched cartoons on the TV. He looked at me and held out the bag of chips. "Want some?" he asked with his mouth full.

"No thanks, I'm good," I said, sitting down on one of the couches. I grabbed the blanket hanging over the side and wrapped it tightly around me. I was still exhausted.

It wasn't long before there was a knock on the door. With the blanket still around me, I got up and walked to the front door, looking through the peephole before opening the door for Logan to come in. He looked even more tired than Flynn did as he walked in and closed the door.

I immediately wrapped my arms around him when the door was locked. "You okay?" I asked in a murmured tone.

Logan sighed. "I already said no."

I led Logan to the living room and he sat down on the chair. I sat on his lap and wrapped the blanket around the both of us before leaning in his chest. "Want to tell me what's wrong now?" I asked.

Logan was silent as he looked at Flynn. Flynn looked back and sighed. "I get it, I get it," Flynn said. "I'll go upstairs."

Once Flynn was upstairs, Logan wrapped his arms tightly around me. "I've been having nightmares," he said. "And....and most of them ends with me losing you. I don't want to lose you, Fin. I love you so much and I can't imagine my life without you."

"You're not going to lose me, Logan," I assured.

"You don't know that," Logan said. "You heard Ryan yourself. The tasks are going to be impossible. We're going to die. It's inevitable."

"Logan, we will survive," I said. "I may not have any hope left, but that doesn't mean I'm just going to give up. You know what happened with my dad. My mom lost him because of this stupid group, and she's not going to lose her two children. We have to make sure of it."

"I can't help but think of it," Logan said. "These nightmares are horrible. The one last night was of a task we had to do. And....you didn't make it. I'm really scared, Infinity. We've been friends for almost ten years and I've been in love with you for so long and if I lost you I...."

I cut him off by pressing my lips on his. When I pulled away, I rested one of my hands on his cheek. "Logan," I said softly. "We're going to make it, okay? Ryan made the wrong choice by involving Flynn because I'm even more determined to survive for him. We're going to make it through this. But I need you to stay strong. Stay strong like you did when we had to do the ten tasks. Stay strong like you did when Ryan was threatening me with a gun, but you tried stopping him. Be strong because of your biceps."

That got Logan to scoff a laugh. "You have an obsession with them, don't you?"

"But of course," I said, holding one of them up. "I mean, look at this thing. Like I've said before, it's like half a grapefruit."

Logan rolled his eyes. "It's not that big, Fin."

"Your biceps are big."

"Okay, fine, they are," Logan said. "You're adorable, you know that?"

"I know," I said, giving him a kiss before smiling at him. "Are you feeling better?"

"Yeah," Logan said. "A bit. You always know how to put a smile on my face, Fin. It's what I love about you."

"You know what I love about you?" I asked.

"My biceps?"

"No," I said. "Well, yes, but what I love most is the fact that you're always there for me. You're the best boyfriend ever. Way better than Toby ever was."

"And you're the best girlfriend," Logan said. "I would say better than my previous girlfriends, but....Yeah."

"Aww, I'm your first girlfriend," I said, squeezing his cheeks. "So cute."

Logan chuckled before wrapping his arms around me and pulling me into a hug. "As annoying as you are, I love you."

"I love you too."

"You know what I love?" Flynn suddenly asked as he walked back into the living room. "Food. Hey, we should get Luke to make food for us."

I rolled my eyes. Luke was our cousin Melody's boyfriend and he was amazing in the kitchen. For the past Christmas, Luke and his brother made a lot of food and Flynn fell in love with it. He didn't leave the buffet table's side.

"Maybe another time," I said.

Flynn sighed before sitting on the couch and grabbing the chips again. "I need a girlfriend."

"That was random," I said.

"What? It's true," Flynn said. "Everyone I know is dating someone."

"And by everyone, you mean me and Logan?" I asked. "Isn't Jake single? And Mike? And basically everyone else you know?"

"Not everyone," I said. "Rebecca isn't."

Logan scoffed at the sound of his younger sister's name. "I still can't believe Becky is dating that jerk," he said.

"Still don't like him?" I asked.

"That's understating it."

I rolled my eyes. "At least he's treating her right."

"Yeah, but...."

He was cut off when there was a sudden beep from the kitchen. Flynn got up and went there, coming back with the cell phone Ryan gave us. He was texting on it with a slight smile.

"Why are you smiling?" I asked.

"Oh, no reason," Flynn said. "Ryan messaged us. He asked if we're ready for the first task."

"Did you say anything back to him?" I asked.

Flynn handed me the cell phone and I widened my eyes. "Flynn!"

"What?" he asked innocently.

I sighed and didn't reply as Ryan replied to Flynn's previous message. Flynn's joking side was going to get the best of him one day.

"Flynn, don't get him mad," I said.

"Oh, come on, it was autocorrect," Flynn said. "Besides, we're all thinking it."

"Thinking it and saying it are two different things," I said, right before Ryan sent another message. The first task, which made me furrow my eyebrows. "Logan, what's this?"

Logan looked at the message before widening his eyes. "Uh....Well, you better not be afraid of heights."

____

Ooh, I wonder what the first task is. cx

I would have had this up sooner, but I was distracted with a game. *cough* My Candy Love *cough* Episode 30 killed me....And now I have to wait for another 2-3 months for the next one....

Oh my gosh, I wrote Luke in here and now I really miss Luke and Melody, and even Jeremy. I want to bring back Jeremy's story soon, but I have way too much books planned out. My stupid imagination. cx

Chapter 8

C hapter 8

Today was the day we had to do the first task and I wasn't up for it at all. It seemed way too dangerous, and this was only the first task. If we made it passed this one, I knew the next ones we going to be impossible.

Ryan wanted us dead, but he didn't want to kill us himself. I hated to admit it, but he was clever.

I quietly put my books in the locker Logan and I shared. He and Flynn were waiting for me and I wasn't going to lie to say that I was stalling.

Lilly happily made her way over to us. I hated not being able to tell her about the tasks. She played such a huge part in the first time we did it. Not only that, but she was my best friend. I couldn't keep secrets from her.

"Why do you all look so glum?" she asked. "Oh....Right. Ryan could come in this city anytime."

If only she knew.

"Well, I know you're all worried, but we should do something today," Lilly said. "Like go to the movies or the fro-yo place."

I sighed. "I wish but...." I didn't really have an excuse and I wasn't that good at making them, so I looked at Flynn for help.

"Social services is coming by today to check to see how everything's going," Flynn said. "They do a check up every six weeks and Mom said that Fin can miss it and we don't know how long it will take."

"Oh," Lilly said before looking at Logan. "And I guess you don't want to do anything without your girlfriend because you're going to get married later on so you have to stick together."

Logan chuckled. "Even when Fin and I are dating, you still aren't letting that go."

"We all know you'll get married," Lilly said. "Well, we can do something tomorrow, right?"

"Yeah, of course," I said in a quiet voice. "We'll see you." When she walked away, I gave Flynn an impressed look. "I didn't know you could lie like that."

Flynn shrugged with a smile. "You do not know how many times I lied at the orphanage to sneak around."

"Ah, like your pickpocket skills," I said.

"Exactly," Flynn said. "So....I guess we have to go. It can't be that bad, right?"

"We'll have to wait and see," Logan said. I closed our locker and the three of us headed to the parking lot and to where Logan's car was parked.

"Logan!" his younger brother suddenly called as he ran up to us. "Can I come?!"

"Uh, we're not going anywhere," Logan said. "I'm taking Fin and Flynn home, then I have to do some errands for Dad."

"I could still come, right?" Jake asked. "I don't want to get in a car with Mike. He's being mean to me."

"Well, you are annoying at times, so I could see why," Logan said.

"Please, Logan?" Jake asked.

Logan sighed. "I'm sorry, Jake. But I have to be alone right now."

"Oh," Jake said, his mood changing to sad. "I get it. I'll see you at home then." He turned around and walked towards their older brother's car.

"I hate lying to him," Logan said as he unlocked the car. We got in and buckled up.

"I know," I said. "I hate lying to my mom and Lilly. I don't get why we can't tell them."

"Because last time when we told people, they were able to help us out," Logan said as he pulled out of the parking lot. "Remember the last task? Because I told my family, they were able to get there in time and treat my and Flynn's wounds. This time, it's going to be harder."

"I guess you're right," I said as he drove towards where Ryan told us to go. It was a good fifteen minute drive and the whole ride was silent.

When we got to the mountain trail, Logan parked his car in an empty spot, but nobody else was there, so it wasn't hard to find a spot.

We got out of the car and Logan locked it before pulling the contact cell phone out of his pocket. "Okay, we have to start heading up this trail," Logan said. "We keep following the trail called...." He sighed at the name. "Graveyard."

I snorted. "Fitting," I muttered under my breath.

"He said to keep following it until we see him," Logan said. "Ryan's already there."

"I still don't get the point of this task," I said as Logan put the phone back in his pocket. "I mean, the last ones we had to do usually had to do with breaking the law or getting the message of Death by Death across. But this?"

"It's dangerous," Flynn spoke up. "If Ryan wants us dead, he won't do the killing himself. It has to look accidental. Let's just go and get this over with." He was then one who started walking up the trail first.

Logan gave me a sympathetic smile before intertwining our hands together and leading me up the trail. I really didn't want to do this, but I had no choice.

We walked for about twenty minutes when we spotted Ryan. He saw us as well and gave us a smirk. "For a minute there, I thought you weren't going to come," he said.

"Yes, because we're totally stupid enough not to do the task and get killed," Flynn said sarcastically, which made Ryan send him a glare as sharp as a knife. Flynn's sarcasm rolled a bit too easily at times, but seeing as he wasn't affected by the glare, he didn't really care.

"You better watch it," Ryan said. "I can make any task as challenging as I want."

Flynn's only reply was a shrug.

"Your task is simple," Ryan said, gesturing to the flat webbing running across the gorge below. "Slacklining is quite fun to me, so it would surely be fun to you."

Not unless we were afraid of heights. I could already see the color draining from Flynn's face. He didn't handle heights that well.

"You will go across this webbing and onto the trail over there," Ryan explained. "Underneath a pile of leaves is a marked x. Dig that up and you'll come across a box that my, uh....let's just say colleague left there when he was on the run. Get that and bring it back. And do not open it up. Now, who will be the one to go?"

The three of us looked at each other. "You mean...." I began.

"Yes, only one of you would be going," he said. "So, who will it be?"

"I will," Logan said, almost immediately. He knew Flynn hated heights and he wanted to keep me safe, even if it meant putting himself in danger.

"Then go ahead," Ryan said. "Oh, and one more thing. There's no safety harness. That would make things a bit too easy."

I carefully made my way over the edge. "That's a long drop."

"I know," Ryan said. "I mean, I could have gotten you three to take the trail over there instead of slacklining, but there's no fun in that. Go ahead, Logan."

Logan took a deep breath before making his way to the webbing. My heart was beating faster for him. There was no safety harness and there drop was really long. If he slipped....

I mentally shook my head. No, think positive. He wouldn't slip. He could do this.

Slowly, Logan stepped onto the webbing, keeping a steady balance. The walk didn't seem that long, but Logan had to take his time if he wanted to keep his balance.

It was so hard for me to watch. With every step he took, I was worried he would lose his footing and fall. There were a few times where he wobbled, but kept a steady balance.

Beside me, Flynn started hyperventilating, his eyes shut tightly. It was probably as hard for him to watch as it was for me.

I sat Flynn on the ground. "Take deep breaths," I told him. "It's okay, Flynn, it's not you on there. You're not going to go on there, so just relax and breath, okay?"

Flynn nodded, pulling his knees to his chest and resting his forehead on it. I kept my arms around him as I turned my focus back to Logan. He was almost on the other side.

Suddenly, Logan began to rock back and forth, finding it hard to keep his balance. It felt like my heart stopped when he lost his balance, but he landed on the other side. I released a breath, trying to calm my rapid heart rate.

Logan found the box and dug it up before setting it beside him and fixing the hole. It was going to be even more challenging coming back while holding the box.

Logan slowly stepped on to the webbing again and made his way back. About halfway, a sharp wind began to blow and it was hard for him to keep his balance. I was trying my best to keep positive thoughts, but it was too hard.

However, the wind slowed down and Logan was able to find his balance. He continued making his way back and when he was safely on the ground, I rushed over to him and wrapped my arms tightly around him, crying softly into his chest. I was so scared and I wasn't even the one on there.

"I'm okay," he said softly, kissing my forehead. Keeping one arm around me, he handed the box to Ryan. "Here."

"Good," Ryan said, taking the box from him. "You were lucky to pass. The next task won't be as easy." With that, he left.

Logan pulled away and helped Flynn stand up. "You okay?" Flynn asked.

Flynn nodded and Logan pulled him in a hug. That was yet another reason why I loved Logan. He always put others in front of himself. What he did was so dangerous, especially without the safety harness, but he was more concerned about how my brother was feeling.

"I just don't get why we couldn't have went on that trail instead of you doing that," Flynn said. "Too bad we don't know what was in the box?"

Logan looked down the trail to where Ryan was walking. When he was out of eyesight, Logan looked at the both of us. "Okay," he said quietly, "I know Ryan told me not to open the box, but I took a quick peak."

"I didn't see you do that," I said.

"Exactly," Logan said. "Anyway, it was a USB, but there has to be something on there that he doesn't want anyone to know about. Why else would his colleague bury it when he was on the run?"

"To hide it from the authorities," I said. "Then what would they be hiding?"

"I don't know, but whatever it is, it can't be good," Logan said.

Here's another chapter! I hope it's quite long, over 1800 words right now. cx

I love Logan a whole lot. He is one of my favorite main characters because of how sweet he is. He was my second main male character I made, and I still love him, even though I love my arrogant boys a whole lot. cx

Chapter 9

C hapter 9

"You what?" Logan asked me. "Are you crazy?"

"I'm not not crazy," I said. "Come on, Logan. Aren't you curious?"

"Curious, yes," Logan agreed. "But I'm not stupid enough to put myself in even more danger. Fin, Ryan specifically told us not to look at what was in the box, but I did anyway. If he finds out that we know about it, I don't even want to think of that consequence."

"But whatever is on the USB can be our ticket to getting out of Death by Death," I said. "Ryan said his colleague hid it while on the run, meaning it's something they don't want the cops seeing."

"It could be instructions for a doomsday device," Flynn suddenly said from being me, making me jump a bit.

"Where did you come from?" I asked.

"Well, one night, my birth parents decided not to use a co--"

"That's not what I meant," I said. "You really need to stop sneaking up on people."

"No thanks," Flynn said. "I'm with you, by the way. About finding out what was on that USB. I think we should do it."

Logan sighed. "Yeah, and get in more trouble?"

"Logan, we're serious," I said.

"Okay, even if we wanted to find out what was on it, how would we?" Logan asked. "Ryan took it and we have no idea where it is."

"Obviously it's somewhere with a computer," Flynn said.

Logan and I both looked at him with furrowed eyebrows.

"What?" Flynn asked. "What would be the point of him taking it if he doesn't have a computer yet? Nobody knew where it was, so he could have well left it there until he had access to a computer."

"That, or he gave it to someone he knows with a computer," I added.

"Exactly," Flynn said. "So all we have to do is find where he's hiding or find out who he gave the USB to."

"Yes, and in the meantime, we can paint huge targets on our faces," Logan said sarcastically.

"Flynn has a point," I said. "Either way, someone with a computer has it and we should find out who."

"And how are we going to do that?" Logan asked.

"Simple," Flynn said. "All known members of Death by Death are listed on this thing called the internet. Have you heard of it?"

Logan rolled his eyes irritably. "Yes, Flynn, I've heard of the internet."

"Then you should know where I'm heading," Flynn said.

"Yes, but you should say what your idea is because Fin probably doesn't get it," Logan said.

I snorted. "Yes. I do not get it. Please explain, dear brother, for the sake of my understanding and not my boyfriend's because he obviously understands."

Flynn raised an eyebrow. "You two have an interesting relationship. Anyway, we look at the list online of members of Death by Death and see their current status. Some are probably in prison, others are hiding, and some could have resigned. All we have to do is find out which one has the USB and if none of them do, then Ryan still has it."

"Or, I have a better idea," Logan said. "We leave it and not care about it. We're back on Death Watch and these tasks are going to be more dangerous, and it's going to be hard enough as it is to survive. If we get caught trying to take the USB...."

"No, just put whatever is on there on another USB," Flynn corrected.

"Okay, if we get caught doing that, I'm pretty sure Ryan will actually kill us," Logan said.

"Not really," Flynn said. "If I recall, when you went to get the box, all he said was 'do not open the box'. Nothing about what will happen if you do. Besides, you opened the box anyway, so I'm sure you'd be down to be rebellious."

Logan looked back and forth between me and Flynn before walking away and out of the school building.

"Well, sis, it looks like it's just me and you," Flynn said.

"Are you sure we should?" I asked. "I mean, Logan does have a point. It is kind of dangerous."

"Okay, then for now, we can just find out some possible people who have the USB," Flynn said. "I wouldn't try getting it so fast, anyway. We need a plan. And possibly help from Jake because he's good at strategy. Video games help with that."

"Flynn, we can't involve Jake," I said. "Ryan told us not to tell anyone, and Logan wouldn't want his little brother involved with all of that. It's hard enough as it is with you being involved."

"Point taken," Flynn said. "How about I don't tell him what it's for? I can....Ooh, he's not in my English class, so I can say I'm writing a short story for class and want it to be as realistic as possible."

"You know, you're actually a very smart person," I said.

"Duh," Flynn said. "Mom's probably waiting for us in the parking lot."

I took my homework out before closing my locker. The two of us headed towards the parking lot and two Mom's car.

As soon as we got home, Flynn pulled my wrist and led me all the way upstairs to my room. He sat at my desk and opened my laptop. "What's the password?" he asked.

"Why can't we use your laptop?" I asked.

"I need a new screen," he said. "I kind of got mad when I was playing Minecraft because a creeper blew up my really awesome house."

"Don't tell me you punched the screen," I said.

"Okay, I won't tell you," Flynn said. "So, password."

I gently pushed him off of my computer chair before sitting down. "I don't trust you on here," I said as I typed in the password. "You tell me what to do, and I'll do it."

"Fine," Flynn said with a dramatic sigh.

For the next two hours, I did everything Flynn told me to do. We got a list of people from Death by Death, as well as the ones in prison, the ones who haven't been seen, and the ones who weren't in Death by Death.

"Now we have to narrow this down," I said. "I don't know how to."

"We'll figure out how," Flynn said. "We don't have to do it today, but at least we have some names. Hey, want to stalk some of these people."

I raised an eyebrow. "You know, I really don't know what goes through your head at times."

"Usually food," he said. "And video games. Speaking of, I'm going to make popcorn and go on the playstation. Peace out, sister." He walked out of my bedroom.

I closed my laptop and set the list of names beside it before heading downstairs as well to eat some food, even though my mom was in the middle of making dinner.

"Infinity, wait until dinner," she said as soon as I opened the fridge.

"But I'm hungry," I said. "I want to eat."

"Which is why you need to wait until dinner," Mom said. "It will be done in ten minute, tops. I even wouldn't allow Flynn to eat popcorn."

"It's a cruel and unusual punishment!" Flynn called from the living room. "I'm a growing boy! I need food!"

"And you will get food in ten minute, tops!" Mom called back before sighing. "I swear, you kids eat too much."

"Because we like food," I said.

"Yeah, I can tell," Mom said. "So, I've been meaning to ask you, how is everything? There is still no sign of Ryan and you seem to be handling it well."

I looked down. I hated not being able to tell my mom that both Flynn and I were basically back on Death Watch. She already lost her husband to it and if Flynn and I didn't want to keep it hidden from her. "Okay, I guess. I've come to learn how to live with it."

"Well, I'm glad to see you holding up strongly," Mom said. "Same with Flynn. I hated having him so quiet, as annoying as he is when he isn't quiet."

"I heard that!" Flynn called.

Mom just smiled and rolled her eyes.

Dinner was ready in ten minutes, so we were soon sitting down and eating at the table. Whenever Mom wasn't looking, Flynn flicked some corn at me, then pretended to act innocent. He was so annoying at times, but honestly, I loved it when he was annoying. It was what brothers did.

When we finished dinner, I did the dishes for my mom so she could finish some paperwork in the office.

While I was washing the dishes, plus more that Flynn kept dirtying, the front door opened all of a sudden, which made me jump. I turned to see Logan rushing towards me. "I found him!" he said.

"Don't do that!" I said. "You scared me!"

"Yeah, yeah, but I found him," he said with a smile.

I furrowed my eyebrows. "Found who?"

"The guy who has the USB," he said.

"What?"

"I found out who has the USB," Logan said.

"How on earth did you find that out?" I asked.

"It took a lot of work," Logan said. "I got all the names of the current and past members of the group. Then I found out the jobs of those who aren't in hiding. One of them works at that huge corporate building in the city beside ours, so I looked up that guy. It turns out that he used to be a close friend of Ryan and also co-founded Death by Death, though he wasn't really known to be the co-founder. That guy, Elvis, was arrested not that long ago, but he got out on good behavior. Then he got a job at that business and got involved in the community."

"So?" I asked. "Wouldn't that mean he isn't associated with Ryan and Death by Death anymore?"

"That's what everyone thinks," Logan said. "But I got Jake to hake into the street cameras near that building and...."

"Wait," I said. "First off, why? And second, how could you convince Jake to do that without telling him about Death by Death."

"I just had to give him a pack of gummy bears, and he'll do anything I ask him to without question," Logan said. "Anyway, I found it kind of weird that he got out on good behavior when he was the co-founder, so that's why I decided to check that building. And, believe or not...." He showed me a picture on his phone of two guys behind the building.

"So?"

Logan sighed and pointed to the one giving the other guy something. He had a baseball cap and sunglasses. "That's Ryan."

"What? How could you tell?"

"Because those were the clothes he wore when we did the first task," Logan said. "And he has a scar on his right hand, which you can see when I zoom in. Fin, this Elvis guy has the USB."

"So basically Flynn and I didn't have to research the names," I said.

"Come on, I'd thought you be more excites," Logan said. "Maybe thank me with a kiss."

I rolled my eyes and gave him a kiss. "Thank you, Logan. I thought you were against us finding out what's on it."

"I was," Logan said. "But I thought about it. What you said about it was right. It has to be something they don't want to cops knowing about and if Death by Death is planning something dangerous, we should at least know about it."

"So, how are we going to get what's on it?" I asked.

"I was thinking about that too," Logan said. "Only one of us should go just in case Ryan's keeping an eye on us."

"And let me guess, you want to go?" I asked.

"Well....yeah."

"Can't I go?" I asked.

"Fin...."

"Logan, I know you want to keep me safe," I said, "but it might make more sense if I go. Think of it this way. If Ryan is keeping an eye on us, he could only watch one house at a time. If he sees you come over and stay inside, he'll think I'm home. Then just bring over Jake and get him and Flynn to do something outside so Ryan knows Flynn is home."

"I guess that makes sense," Logan said. "We just have to figure out how to get what's on there."

"Don't worry," I said. "Flynn and Jake play a lot of video games, so this is their specialty." Logan opened his mouth to say something, but I kept talking. "And Flynn is already going to tell him that it's for a short story."

"Okay," Logan said hesitantly. "I guess we're going to find out what's on the USB."

I smiled and kissed his cheek. "And don't worry, I'll make sure I stay safe when I go. We'll even talk via cell phone or something."

Logan nodded and smiled faintly. "You know, for once, I actually think we're going to survive this."

"Me too," I said.

———————————

Yay! This chapter is actually pretty long! cx I think I have a good idea as to where this book is going and school is almost finished, so updates should come more often. However, I'm focusing on another book right now first, but the updates for this won't be as slow.

One reason why I feel better for writing this is the cast. I am officially in love with Brenton Thwaites because of a movie I watched, so I casted him as Logan and now I'm just imagining Brenton and it makes me happy. cx

Chapter 10

C hapter 10

"I'm still not sure about you going to get what's on that USB," Logan said, pulling me closer. "What if you get caught?" My head was rested on his chest and one of his arms were around me.

"And what if we don't find out what's on it?" I asked. "What if it's something that they'll use against everyone?"

"I know," Logan said. "And I know it's important to find out what's on it, but I don't want you to risk yourself. I can do it."

"And have you risk yourself?" I asked, tracing circles with my finger on his bare chest. "We already talked about it. It's best for me to do it."

Logan sighed. "I know, but....You know I hate the idea of you getting into a dangerous situation."

"I could say the same thing for you," I said. "Logan, I really love you, but you can't expect to risk yourself just to keep me and Flynn safe. We're in this together."

"I know, but...."

"But nothing," I said. "It won't be fair for you to keep risking yourself. You already did the first task by yourself and that was extremely hard for me to watch."

"Fin," Logan said, propping himself on his elbows. "Your mom already lost her husband to Death by Death. Do you really want her to lose her children?"

"And do you really want me to lose you?" I asked. "Logan, all we have to do is work together. No risking ourselves."

Logan sighed. "I know. I just can't help it. I love you so much and I can't stand the thought of you, or even Flynn, getting hurt." He stroked my cheek with his thumb before resting his hand on it. "Promise you won't get hurt?"

"I can't promise anything in our situation," I said. "But I will try my hardest not to get hurt. Same with you. You'll try not to get hurt, right?"

Logan gave me a thin smile. "Just for you, I'll try." He pressed a kiss onto my nose before laying back down beside me. "So when are we doing the whole USB thing?"

"Once our brothers find out exactly how I will get in there and do it," I said. "It shouldn't take that long, though. Flynn is imagining it like it's some video game, which he loves. And when Flynn and Jake play video games together, it turns really serious."

"Yeah, I know," Logan said. "Once when Flynn was over, they were playing a game and when I told them it was dinner, they both yelled and threw a pillow at me and Flynn even through a can of soda at me. Needless to say, my parents won't let Flynn and Jake have soda anymore."

I snorted. "Yeah, that sounds like my brother. Let me guess, the soda sprayed everywhere."

"Oh yeah," Logan said. "It got all over me, the floor, the walls. You know, speaking of soda, I'm quite thirsty and hungry. Can we order in some pizza or something?"

"Sure," I said. "Meat lover pizza?"

"You know me so well," Logan said. He gave me a quick kiss before reaching over the side of the bed and grabbing our clothes. We put them on before heading downstairs and into the kitchen. I grabbed the phone off of the counter and ordered the pizza before we went to the living room to watch a movie.

Not long after we were sitting on the couch, the front door opened and both Flynn and Jake came in. "Guess what?" Flynn asked after he and Jake were in the living room. "We did it."

"Did what?" I asked.

"Figured out my short story," Flynn said. "I really think I'm going to get an A."

Jake snorted. "Are you still going on with the whole short story thing? Because I think we both know it's a lie."

"What?" Flynn asked. "I would never lie to my best friend."

"Logan, is Flynn lying to me?" Jake asked. "I feel like he's lying to me."

"Hey, Fin and I ordered pizza," Logan said. "Meat lovers. And since it's my favorite, we got two boxes, plus some soda. You two can have some if you don't spray me with soda."

Jake frowned. "And now you're avoiding the question. What's really going on? Lately, I feel like the three of you have been hiding something from me."

"We're not hiding anything," Flynn said.

"Yeah, sure," Jake said. "Logan asked me to hack into the street camera outside of a building and you needed my help with a short story about someone by the name of Quinn going into a building to get a USB."

"And?" Flynn asked.

"Quinn rhymes with Fin," Jake pointed out. "If you're going to lie, pick a different name."

Flynn sighed. "Okay, here's the deal. We...."

"We can't tell you," Logan interrupted. "Not if we want to keep you safe, Jake."

"It has to do with that guy that's after you, right?" Jake asked. When neither of us responded, he knew the answer. "Then why does Flynn get to know?"

I looked over at Logan. Jake was going to keep getting curious and hiding things from him would only make things worse.

Logan knew what I was trying to silently tell him, because he sighed in reply and looked at his younger brother. "Okay, we can't tell you everything," he said. "But yes, the whole USB thing has to do with that guy that is after us. We think something dangerous is on it and if we at least know what it is, then it might help us."

"Then why didn't you just say so?" Jake asked.

"Because I don't want to risk you getting in trouble," Logan said. "Things are so tough right now and the last thing I want is for you getting involved."

"Can I at least have a pack of gummy bears?" Jake asked.

"I just got you some," Logan said.

"Yeah, and I finished it," Jake said.

Logan sighed. "Fine, I'll get you another one."

"So," Flynn said. "Since we figured out the whole plan, when are we going to do it?"

"Tomorrow," I said.

Logan looked at me with a raised eyebrow. "Tomorrow? But...."

"Don't push the day back," I said. "No matter what, it's going to happen. We should get it done and over with."

"Okay," Logan said. "So, geniuses, how does the plan work?"

———————————

It's been so hot here for the past couple days and I hate it. I like the cold more than the heat. cx

So, I am rewriting the first book because I wasn't satisfied with it, so these updates might start coming slowly again. I don't want to get too far in this book and have to rewrite it in the future because it doesn't match up with the rewritten version of Stay By My Side.

And now, here's a gif of Loganity just because:

Chapter 11

C hapter 11

"Logan, I'm serious, let me go," I said.

"But if I do, something bad might happen," Logan said, his arms wrapping tighter around me.

I sighed. "It has to be done, Logan. We have to know what's on there."

"Then I'll go," he said. "I'll go and do it and...."

"No," I said. "You can't keep risking yourself. It's already been planned that I'm doing it, okay?"

Logan sighed, resting his chin on top of my forehead and continued hugging me. I let him hug me for a bit longer.

Flynn and Jake came down the stairs. "Infinity, are you going to leave yet?" Flynn asked. "We have to get this done before the man Ryan gave the USB gets off of his break and he's going on it soon."

"I would, be someone won't let go of me," I said.

"Logan, let go," Flynn said. "You're making me mad because I can't hug Lilly because she won't accept our relationship and I need her in my life."

I sighed. "Flynn, give it up."

"Never," Flynn said. "I'll be you one hundred bucks that Lilly and I will get together....eventually."

I rolled my eyes and locked up at Logan. "Can you let me go now?" I asked. "I really have to go."

Logan finally released me, but then he pressed his lips on mine. "Okay, go," he said. "Be careful."

"Wait," Jake said before handing me an earpiece. "Call us when you get there and talk on this. We'll monitor everything on my laptop and tell you what to do."

"Got it," I said. I kissed Logan's cheek. "I'll be fine."

I was about to walk out through the backyard, but Logan grabbed my wrist and pulled me back to him, wrapping his arms around me. "Be safe," he muttered.

I chuckled. "I will," I said. "Logan, this isn't even dangerous at all. I'm just going there to find out what's on the USB. That's it." I kissed his cheek again before walking out of the house through the backdoor.

I walked behind the back of the houses for a bit before going onto the side walk and making my way to the building where I had to get the USB. It really shouldn't be that hard. All I had to do was go in, act like I belonged there, waited for the man to go on break, get in his office and download the files onto my USB, then get out.

Okay, that was a lot to do, but it still shouldn't be hard.

I got to the building and luckily, that wasn't a place to sign in or anything. I called Logan's cell number on my phone before hooking it up to the earpiece. "Can you come home now?" was the first thing Logan asked.

"No," I said. "We need to get this done. Is he on his break yet?"

"Not yet," Logan said. "He's about to in about two minutes so head up to the floor below his. There's a washroom there that you can stay in until it's safe for you to go onto his office floor."

"Got it," I said. "And....What floor is his office on?"

"Uh....Seven," Logan said. "So go to the sixth floor, head straight, and the washrooms will be on the right."

"Okay," I said before heading there.

Since nobody else was in the washroom, I just had to stand there for a bit until Logan told me it was safe to go to the man's office. I followed his directions to get there and when I did, I sighed. "The computer needs a password," I said. "I don't know the password."

"Okay, hold on," Logan said. He talked to Jake for a bit. "Um, Jake said to try looking for a post-it note with the password on."

I snorted, but I began looking. "Why would he have a post-it note, saying what his password is? Wouldn't he, like, save it on his phone or even remember it?"

"Just keep looking," Logan said.

"Okay, but...." I found a post-it note just then and took the chance, typing it into the laptop. "Well. I'm in."

"Shouldn't I be saying that?" Logan asked, and I knew he had a smile on his face.

"Shut up," I said, opening one of the drawers, but there were way too many USBs. "What did the USB look like?"

"It was black," he said. "Plain black."

"That doesn't help," I said. "Most of them are."

"Hold on, let me remember," Logan said. "Oh, it had a chip on the paint."

I dug through the drawer, finding only one with a chip on it. I put it into the computer before taking out the USB in my pocket, plugging it into the computer. "There's only one document on here," I said. "It says confidential."

"Suspicious enough," Logan said. "You've got to quickly put it onto our USB. Depending how big the document is, it can take a while and you don't have that much time left."

I dragged the folder into our USB folder, copying it in there. I had to wait for a bit before it was fully completed.

"Uh, Fin, you've got to get out of there," Logan said. "He's on his way back up."

I quickly unplugged the USB's, making sure to put mine back in my pocket and his back in the drawer. I closed it and logged off of the computer. "Done," I said.

"You're going to have to take the stairs," Logan said. "He's in the elevator and there's a huge chance that he knows what Infinity Cooper looks like."

I sighed. "Great, so I have to take the stairs?"

"Yes, that's what I said," Logan said. "Just hurry up, babe."

"Don't call me babe," I said as I made my way to the stairs. I then had to go down all six flights of stairs, making my way to the entrance. "I'm out of the building. I told you it wasn't dangerous."

"Okay, you told me," Logan said. "I'll see you soon."

"Yeah, see you," I said.

When I got back home, walking inside through the backdoor. Logan immediately pulled me into a hug. "You're okay," he said.

"Of course I am," I said. "It wasn't hard."

"Logan, stop being too lovey-dovey," Flynn said. "Seriously. You saw her on the footage. She was fine."

"I know," Logan said before kissing my forehead.

We then walked over to Jake and I handed him the USB. He plugged it into the the computer and opened up the file. "No. Way."

"What is it?" Logan asked.

"Something dangerous," Jake said. "If Death by Death is planning on building this....We're not safe."

———————————

Ooh, I wonder what it is. cx

It feels good to write this book again. I have a lot of twists and turns planned for the book. :)

Chapter 12

C hapter 12

Lilly walked into the house, not even bother knocking. "Movie night!" she announced. "I feel like we haven't done anything for a while, just the five of us." She walked into the living room where we were sitting, immediately frowning. "Why do you all look sad? Come on, it's movie night!"

"Yay, movie night," Jake said in a monotone. "Woo hoo. Fun."

Lilly sighed and sat down on the couch beside Flynn. "I got a new shirt, Flynn," she said, gesturing to the shirt she was wearing. "What do you think?"

"Oh, it's nice," Flynn said.

Lilly frowned. "It's nice? That's it?" she asked.

Flynn just shrugged before he began fiddling with his thumbs.

"Can someone tell me why you're all so sad?" Lilly asked.

I looked over at Logan, silently asking if we should tell Lilly what was going on. And Jake, because he didn't know all of it. He just knew about the USB and what was on it.

Besides, how was Ryan going to find out if we tell anyone? Especially if Lilly and Jake acted like they didn't know.

Logan nodded before we looked back at Lilly. "Okay, we'll tell you," he said. "And Jake, we'll tell you the whole story."

"But...." Flynn said.

"It will be fine," Logan assured. "So Ryan is actually in the town. He found me and Infinity but instead of killing us like we thought he would, he decided to give us ten more tasks, and he said they're most likely going to be impossible. But that's not all. Flynn was with us when Ryan found us and he has to do the tasks with us."

"But that's not fair!" Jake said.

"I know," Logan said. "That's not all. The first task we had to do was retrieve a box, and he told us not to look inside. I did anyway and it was a USB."

"The one that we found out what was on it," Jake said.

"Yeah," Logan said.

"What was on it?" Lilly asked.

"Directions," Logan said. "To make a gas bomb out of sarin gas. The gas is highly toxic and can kill someone within ten minutes, and the death is torturous."

"You think Death by Death is planning on building it?" Lilly asked.

"That's what we're guessing," I said. "We don't know where they'll use it but no matter what, people are going to die."

Logan put his arm around my shoulder and gave me a side hug. "I never thought they would take it this far," he said. "I know they're dangerous people, but mass killing? That's a while other story."

"So, what are we going to do about it?" Lilly asked.

"We don't know," I said. "Right now, we're just moping."

"Yeah, that I can see," Lilly said. "Because a certain someone hasn't flirted with me yet." She then frowned. "And he said my shirt was nice."

"It is nice," Flynn said, which made Lilly punch his arm. "Ow! What was that for?!"

"Flynn, rule number one of girls," Logan said. "Never say something is nice. Unless you want to die."

Flynn shrugged. "Hey, Lilly, Jake and I were talking earlier and we got into an argument about the alphabet. There's twenty letters in the alphabet, right?"

"No, there's twenty-six," Lilly said. "Are you that stupid?"

"No," Flynn said. "I must have forgotten U R A Q T."

"Funny," Lilly said. "You're still forgetting one."

"I know," Flynn said. "I'll give you the D later." He then winked at her.

"Flynn!" Lilly said, punching his shoulder again. "I can't believe you!"

"What? You're the one who wanted me to flirt with you."

"I....I did not say that."

"You implied it," Flynn said.

"You kind of did," Jake spoke up.

Lilly glared at Flynn before getting up from the couch and moving to sit on the chair instead. "I am never going near you again, Flynn," she said.

"I'm sorry," Flynn said. "By the way, I lost my teddy bear. Can I sleep with you tonight?"

Lilly's reply was to throw a pillow at Flynn and glared at him. Flynn was never going to give up flirting with Lilly. I felt bad for her.

But at the same time, it was kind of hilarious.

Lilly chose a movie to watch, and Flynn went to the kitchen with Jake to make some popcorn and get some soda as well. The shortly came back with three bowls of popcorn; one for me and Logan to share, one for Jake and Flynn to share, and one just for Lilly.

Which Lilly chose to waste by throwing some at Flynn throughout the movie. Which only made Flynn throw it back. Then flirt with her.

I rolled my eyes and scooted closer to Logan, resting my head on his shoulder. He squeezed my shoulder and kissed my forehead before resting his head on mine. "You worried about Death by Death?" he asked in a quiet voice.

"Yeah," I said, my voice as quiet. "If they build it and if they use it...."

Logan sighed. "I know. But right now, we have to focus on finishing the tasks."

"It's kind of hard when all along, Death by Death will most likely be building the gas bomb," I said, intertwining my hand in his.

"I know," he said. "But the least we can do is complete the tasks. Once we're free from Death by Death, we'll be able to do what we want, including helping the police find them." He looked at me, giving me a small smile.

"We'll make it through this, okay? We're going to try our hardest and we will survive."

I smiled back at him, but it felt a bit weak. "Okay."

Logan gave me a quick but sweet kiss before resting his head back on mine and turning to the movie. I couldn't really focus on it. I was too distracted thinking about the weapon Death by Death was planing on building. They were going from targeting one person to targeting who knows how many.

Our situation got a whole lot more serious.

———————————————

Sorry for not updating for a while. I'll try to get back to the regular schedule of updating.

I love Flynn so much. cx He's bae.

And here is a random gif of Loganity to brighten the mood of this chapter:

Chapter 13

C hapter 13

We have been waiting for a few days now to get the next task and I was nervous as hell. I was worried that they were actually going to build the gas bomb. We had to do something about it, but we were just teens.

There had to be something we could do.

"Mom!" Flynn called from the living room. "I'm heartbroken!"

"Why?" Mom asked, walking into the living room.

"I asked out a girl today, and she said no," Flynn said. "It was heartbreaking."

I rolled my eyes. "And let me guess. It was Lilly?" I asked.

"What?" Flynn asked. "No, of course not....Okay, it might have been Lilly. Don't worry, one day, she will be my girlfriend."

"Keep dreaming," I said. I highly doubt that Lilly would agree to date Flynn.

"Stop being mean to me," Flynn said. "Mom, I need some ice cream to feel better. I'm really heartbroken and I don't know if I'll ever get over it."

Mom just sighed and shook her head before walking back into the kitchen.

"You really need to get over Lilly," I said. "She's three years older than you."

"Shut up," Flynn said. "She's the love of my life."

I ignored him, mainly because I heard the Death by Death cell phone buzz on the coffee table. I sighed, picking it up and reading the message. I frowned before grabbing my own phone and calling Logan. I told him that we had another task and had to leave as soon as we could, so he told me he would be on his way.

"We have another task?" Flynn asked when I hung up my phone.

"Yeah," I said. "I'll explain everything in the car." I then went to the kitchen where Mom was baking cookies. "Mom, Logan's going to come pick me and Flynn up, then we're going to go to out somewhere. I feel like we've been stuck inside all day."

"Okay," Mom said. "Make sure you're careful. I know you don't like to think about it, but that man can show up at anytime."

"I know," I said in a quiet voice. "We'll be careful."

"Good," Mom said, giving me a thin smile.

I walked back out of the kitchen and Flynn and I got ready to leave. It wasn't long before Logan pulled into the driveway, so we got into his car.

"So, what's the task?" Logan asked.

"We have to go to this place and get a can with this symbol on it," I said, showing Logan the text with the symbol attached.

Logan sighed. "And where is the location?"

I got the directions and put it on the GPS before Logan began driving there. "Logan? Do you know what the symbol is?" I asked.

"Well, if I were to take a wild guess, I'd say it is sarin gas," he said.

"You really think they're planning on making the gas bomb?" I asked.

"Why else would they want those directions back?" Logan asked. "They would have kept it there until they're ready to build it."

"And I guess they're going to get us to get all the supplies," Flynn spoke up. "So they don't get caught."

I sighed and rubbed my forehead. "What was Ryan thinking when he decided to make this group? How can someone ever want to kill innocent people?"

"I don't know, Fin," Logan said. "I really don't. I'm just hoping we get out of this."

"And find a way to stop the gas bomb," Flynn said. "I don't know how."

"At least we have instructions to make it," I said. "I don't know if it would help, but we'll know what we're dealing with."

"Let's make it ourselves and drop it on their HQ," Flynn said.

"Flynn, no," I said. "We're not going to stoop to their level."

Flynn sighed. "I know."

It took a while to get to the place, which looked like an abandon warehouse. I had no idea how we were going to easily get the can if there was security. Hopefully there wasn't.

We got out of the car and carefully walked toward the backdoor. Logan opened it for me and Flynn and as soon as we got in, we were met with a long hallway with dozens of doors. Great.

"Now what?" Flynn asked.

"Look?" Logan asked. "This could take forever and we might get caught."

"What does the symbol look like?" Flynn asked. I showed Flynn a picture of the symbol. "Ooh, I know where it is."

"How would you know where it is?" I asked.

"These signs on the door," Flynn said, pointing to one of the doors. "This one is non-toxic gases, so I'm guessing we have to find the door with that sign. Easy."

"Yeah, so easy," Logan said. "You know, if we don't get caught and jailed."

"Be optimistic," Flynn said as he started walking down the hallway. It wasn't long before he found it and without hesitation, he opened the door and walked in.

I swear, one day, he was going to get into a lot of trouble.

He then walked back out, carrying a can with an identical symbol to the one Ryan sent us. "Got it," he said. "That was easy."

"Yeah," Logan said. "A bit too easy. Isn't anyone else worried about how there's literally no security?"

"Who cares?" Flynn asked. "We should just leave before anyone finds out."

We left the building and as soon as we did, a loud blaring filled through the air, as well as red flashing lights blinking on the outside. Flynn immediately started running to the car and since I was bit hesitant, Logan grabbed my hand and pulled me to the car.

We quickly got inside and Logan pulled out of the parking lot. I quickly messaged Ryan, telling him that we got the can. He gave us a meeting place, so I told Logan where.

"You think we were noticed?" Logan asked.

"Hopefully not," I said.

"It still was pretty easy," Flynn said. "It's not our fault they have a lack of security."

"Tell me about it," Logan said.

The car then went into silence, so I turned on the radio, which was a big mistake because Flynn started "singing" loudly. And by that, I meant screaming at the top of his lungs.

When we got to the place to meet Ryan, Flynn handed Logan the can because Logan offered to quickly drop it off.

He shortly came back and climbed into the driver's seat. "He said the next one's going to be easier," Logan said.

"Good, because this one was very easy," Flynn said. "I bet it's some more materials for the bomb."

"I wouldn't doubt it," Logan said.

I hate that I know what I want to write, but I can't bring myself to actually write the chapter. :/

I don't even have an idea on where this book is going. cx I have the ending planned out, but that's it.

Chapter 14

- -

C hapter 14

At lunch, I waled to the normal table I sat at in the cafeteria. Logan was already sitting down, his head resting on the table as his quiet snores sounded. I chuckled and sat down beside him, seeing the bags under his eyes. He must have been really tired to be able to sleep in the loud cafeteria.

Lilly sat down across from us. "Aww, he looks so cute when he's asleep," Lilly said as if she was talking to a baby. "Why is he asleep anyway?"

I shrugged. "Beats me. He usually gets a lot of sleep at night."

"Except for when you sleep together," Lilly said. "Wink wink."

I sighed. "You're really annoying at times."

"It's my duty as a best friend," Lilly said with a smile.

I rolled my eyes and began eating my chicken ranch wrap. I was going to wake Logan up so he could pay attention to me, but I wasn't too mean to not let him sleep.

Flynn and Jake sat down at the table as well, with Flynn sitting between the two of them. "Hey, Lilly," Flynn said. "Want to go out Friday night?"

Lilly sighed irritably. "No. And stop asking me out. I'm too old for you."

"Age is just a number," Flynn said.

"Yeah? And jail is just a place," Lilly said.

"You'll want me eventually," Flynn said, taking a bite out of his pasta.

"Or never," Lilly said.

"Sure," Flynn said in a sarcastic way. I sighed and rolled my eyes. Poor Lilly, always a target of Flynn's flirting.

Logan was still asleep, so I looked over at Jake. "Do you know why he's so tired?" I asked.

"Beats me," Jake said. "I fell asleep really early last night, so I don't know if he stayed up."

"I can wake him up for you," Flynn said.

"No, just let h--"

Flynn didn't even listen to me. Instead, he decided to yell Logan's name, causing Logan to jump awake. He then sighed, rubbing his forehead. "Thank you for that, Flynn," Logan said sarcastically.

"You're welcome," Flynn said, either not knowing Logan was being sarcastic or he was just ignoring it.

"Are you okay?" I asked Logan, gently rubbing his shoulder.

"Yeah," he said. "I'm just really tired. I was up all night trying to find something that will....will be a thing for that....that thing."

"I need a translation," I said.

"Hmm?" Logan asked.

"Are you sure you'll be okay to go to the rest of the classes?" I asked. "You're really tired."

"What classes?" he asked.

"Okay, I'm going to bring me over to my house," I said. "Gimme your car keys."

Logan reached into his backpack and grabbed his car keys. Once they were in my hand, he laid his head back down on the table. I sighed. Taking care of a tired Logan was not going to be fun.

"Logan," I said. He looked up at me with a tired look. "Come on, I'm going to take you to my house to rest."

"Oh. Right."

"I didn't know you could drive," Flynn said as Logan stood up from the table, grabbing his backpack as well.

"I have my license," I said. "We just can't afford another car right now. Now if you'll excuse me, I am going to take my very tired boyfriend to a place where he can rest."

"I'm guessing you're not going to be back," Lilly said with a frown. "Don't leave me here with these two."

"Sorry," I said. "Flynn? Don't hit on Lilly."

"I'm going to pretend I didn't hear that," Flynn said.

I sighed and grabbed Logan's arm, as well as my bag and my lunch, before leading him outside and to his car. I got into the driver's seat as Logan got in the passenger seat, immediately finding a comfortable position and closing his eyes.

I started up the car and drove to my house. I didn't think Mom would like me coming home in the middle of the day, but Logan seemed really tried but also looked like he didn't want to be left alone. I was lucky when I remembered Mom was working today.

When we got to my house, I grabbed my stuff and helped Logan get out of the car. He was probably going to pass out any minute.

We got inside my house and took of our shoes. Logan dropped his bag on the ground before flopping onto the couch, immediately falling asleep. I, on the other hand, just sat on the couch and continued eating the delicious spicy chicken wrap.

After I finished, I was still hungry, so I went to the kitchen and poured some chips into a bowl before going back to the living room.

While I was eating the chips, Logan ended up waking up from his very short nap. "Fin?" he asked in a tired voice. "How did I get here?"

I chuckled. "You forget a lot of things when you're tired. I took you here because you looked extremely tired during lunch. You still look tired."

Logan sighed and rubbed his eyes. "I am. Cuddle with me?"

I smiled at him and set the bowl of chips onto the coffee table before climbing onto the couch with Logan. In fact there wasn't enough room so I was basically laying on top of him.

"So why were you up at night?" I asked as he wrapped his arm around me. "You said you were looking for something that will be a thing for the thing."

Logan sighed. "Well, since Death by Death is most likely creating that gas bomb, I was trying to find something that can serve as a sort of antidote for anyone that gets affected by it."

"That's a smart idea," I said. "Did you find anything?"

"I would have told you right away if I did," Logan said. "I'm still looking for it though. I'm not going to give up. I don't want Death by Death to win whatever battle they're wanting to fight."

———————————

I WISH I HAD MORE IDEAS FOR THIS. *tear*

I have the ending planned, just nothing for before that. This will probably even be shorter than all of my other books but never fear, because Flynn gets a book. :D He'll be 18 though, but he'll still be Flynn.

Chapter 15

- -

C hapter 15

Logan

Even though my family was quite worried about me ever since that news broadcast of Ryan saying he was out to get me and Fin, our family was still crazy, especially since all four of us teenagers were living in the house.

That was a main reason I was always at Fin's house. It was refreshing to have space for once.

While we were eating dinner, we were all talking about random things. Well, except Jake. He was busy pushing around the corn on his plate. Dad noticed and looked at him with a raised eyebrow. "Jake, stop playing with your food and eat," he said.

"I don't like corn," Jake muttered.

"Don't be ridiculous," Dad said. "You always say as long as it's edible, you'll eat it."

"That doesn't mean I like it," Jake said.

"Then eat the other food on your plate," Dad said.

Jake sighed deeply before stabbing a piece of chicken and taking a tiny bite out of it. I was the only one that knew what was going on with Jake because out of everyone, he trusted me the most.

"So, Logan," Dad said. "Your mother and I have been meaning to talk to you."

"If it's about the whole Death by Death thing, I'd rather not talk about it," I said.

"It's not about that," Mom said. "It's about Infinity."

"No," I said. "No, please don't do this in front of everyone."

Mom chuckled. "Not that talk, Logan. We all know you do it anyway."

"Mom!"

"What?" Mom asked. "I'm right, aren't I?"

I rested my head on the table, feeling my cheeks burning. "Why would you say that?" I then looked up. "Fellow siblings, I advise you never get a girlfriend or a boyfriend."

"Yeah, I know," Rebecca said, crossing her arms and leaning back in her chair. "Dominic broke up with me because apparently, I'm too immature for him."

"He what?" Mike asked. "Do you want me to beat him up for you?"

"Yes," Rebecca said.

"No," Dad said. "I told you, you guys aren't allowed to get into fights. Rebecca chose to date him, so she has to learn that not all relationships last."

Rebecca rolled her eyes. "Yeah, yeah, you already gave me that lecture. Not all relationships last. You have to make sure it's the person you want to marry, yada yada yada."

"Hey, if you want an idea of a perfect relationship, just look at Logan and Infinity," Mike said, giving my shoulder a punch.

I shrugged and took a bite of a piece of chicken. What's right is right.

"Which reminds me," Dad said. "Logan, you really need to stop spending so much time at Infinity's house."

"Wait, that's what you wanted to talk to me about her?" I asked. "Why?"

"You're there almost every day," Mom said.

"Yeah, and?" I asked. "She's my best friend and my girlfriend, and you and Dad both know what we're going through. We'd rather be together to figure all this crap out."

"Language, Logan," Dad warned.

I snorted. "I wouldn't consider crap a curse word. I've heard worse things come out of Mike's mouth."

"Hey, he's right," Mike said. "About both things. Come on, this dangerous man is out to get Logan and Infinity. Of course they're going to spend all their time together."

"Yeah, and speaking of, I'm heading over there after dinner," I said. "Game night she and Lilly are planning." I then looked over at Jake. "You going to come?"

"Uh, no," Jake said. "I've got homework. A lot of homework."

I raised an eyebrow. "Homework? On Friday? You always do it Sunday night."

Jake gave me with a sort of sad look, then looked back at his plate of food.

"Right," I said.

"Jake, are you okay?" Mom asked. "You've been quieter than usual, and that definitely says something."

"I'm fine," Jake said. "I'm just....tired, I guess."

"You guess?" Mom asked.

Jake shrugged and went back to poking at his food with his fork. I tried getting to tell our parents what was going on, but he was too afraid to. I understood. I mean, Dad could be judgmental at times. He would probably be upset or made with Jake at first, but I knew he would eventually accept it.

Saying it wasn't that easy, either. It wasn't like Jake could simply say, 'Hey, Mom and Dad. I'm pansexual and I have a crush on my best friend.'

When dinner finished, I got ready to head over to Fin's house. I asked Jake again if he wanted to come, but he didn't.

I drove to Fin's house and walked in without knocking. They got so used to me coming over the Fin's mom actually gave me a key for the door.

"Aww, where's Jake?" Flynn asked.

"He has homework," I said as I took of my shoes, then sat down beside Fin on the couch.

"That's lame," Flynn said. "Homework should be banned. I mean, we already spend six hours at school. We don't need more time in our day to do work."

"Then you should tell the teachers that," Fin said.

"I tried," Flynn said. "They either gave me more homework, or told me that homework is 'essential'. So, game night time. Since Jake isn't here, we should do couples game night."

Lilly sighed. "For the last time, we are not a couple, nor will we ever be."

"You say that now, but Infinity has also said that she won't date Logan because they're only best friends," Flynn pointed out. "And look how happily in love they are, just like how we will be happily in love."

"Shut up," Lilly said. "How about we do boys against girls since there's two of each?"

"Did you just assume my gender?" Flynn asked.

"You know, I come here often to get away from my crazy family," I said. "You're not really helping."

"Hey, I haven't had any siblings for thirteen years," Flynn said. "Now that I have a sister, I have to be as annoying as I could possibly be. I'm going to get some food. Want to help me, Lilly?"

"I'm only helping you because you never bring the soda I want," Lilly said as she stood up.

"What? I always bring you your favorite soda," Flynn said.

"No. No you don't."

"Your favorite soda is Diet Coke. I always bring that."

"I don't remember you ever doing so."

Flynn huffed as he walked to the kitchen with Lilly following.

"So...." Fin said. "What's really going on with Jake? I know for a fact that he's against doing homework on Fridays, and he has always been so quiet."

Jake kind of figured that I would tell Fin about him since I told her everything, and he told me he was okay with it so long as she didn't tell anyone. Luckily, unlike Flynn, Fin never told anyone secrets.

"So, Jake kind of has a crush on Flynn," I said. "He's pansexual, and he's trying to avoid him until the feelings go away since we all know Flynn likes Lilly."

"Oh," Fin said. "Well, if it makes him feel any better, Flynn doesn't have a chance with Lilly."

"I don't know, I think she likes him and won't admit it," I said.

"What? No way," Fin said.

"Come on, she's always asking his opinion on her clothes," I said. "And Flynn was right. He always brings her Diet Coke, so she was just using that as an excuse to help him out."

"Okay, but that doesn't mean she likes him," Fin said.

"Uh huh, whatever you say," I said.

––––––––––––––––––––

Lol, I always read your comments and sometimes, I go with your ideas. cx Like, someone started shipping Flynn and Lilly, so now I do, and another person wanted Jake to have a crush on either Flynn or Lilly, so I did that. cx Jake is officially my first pansexual character. :D

But seriously, who couldn't have a crush on Flynn?

I WANT MORE IDEAS FOR THIS BOOK SO I COULD START WRITING THE FLYLLY BOOK. D: I have little to no ideas for this except for the ending and trust me, the ending is going to be epic. :D

Chapter 16

C hapter 16

"You know what I realized," I said to Logan, pausing the movie we were watching and turning to face him. "That we haven't gotten a task in a while."

Logan groaned. "No, don't say that. Usually when one of us brings up the fact that we haven't done a task in a while, we end up doing a test shortly."

"Those were coincidences," I said. "I'm serious, though. I'm happy we haven't done anything. Remember that he said they're going to be really dangerous?"

Logan snorted. "Dangerous? We did two and both of them weren't dangerous."

I raised an eyebrow. "Um, you do remember the first one, right? When you had to walk on that rope without a harness or a net underneath?"

"Well, yeah, but I finished it," Logan said. "Therefore, it wasn't dangerous."

"Do you even know the definition of dangerous?" I asked.

"No, of course not," Logan said sarcastically. "Even though I have the highest GPA in school and everyone made fun of me for being a nerd, I don't know the definition of all."

I just smiled at him and kissed his cheek. "If it's any consolation, you were a very cute nerd."

"I'm still cute," Logan said.

"That, you are," I said. "So....How's Jake doing? It's kind of weird not having him here hanging out with Flynn and being all weird."

"Yeah, I know," Logan said. "He's doing okay. He knows he doesn't have a chance with Flynn because we all know Flynn and Lilly will be a couple eventually."

"What?" I asked. "No way."

"Yes way," Logan said. "You know she likes him."

I snorted. "Yeah, right. Lilly liking my younger brother?"

"You see the way she's always asking his opinion on the clothes she wears," Logan said. "And how she indirectly asks for him to flirt with her."

"Yeah, I still don't think she likes him," I said.

"She totally does."

"Okay, keep thinking that," I said.

"I will because it's true. You just don't want to accept it."

"I'm not accepting it because it's not true. I think Lilly, one of my best friends, would tell me if she liked someone."

"Not really, not," Logan said. "Not everyone would tell their best friend if they like someone. Take Jake for example. You really think he's going to tell his best friend that he likes him?"

"What?" a voice came nearby.

Logan and I looked over, seeing Flynn standing by the stairs. "Uh, hey, Flynn," Logan said. "So, any new games you've been playing?"

"Jake likes me?" Flynn asked.

"What? No," Logan said. "No, not you. Jake's....other best friend."

"He doesn't have any other best friends, as sad as that is," Flynn said.

"What about....that girl?"

"Logan, stop trying to avoid what you just said," Flynn said. "I heard you. You said Jake likes his best friend, and you said it was a him. Is that why he doesn't come over anymore? Because he likes me?"

Logan sighed and rubbed his forehead. "You did not hear that from me. In fact, you didn't hear it at all. Just forget I didn't say anything, okay?"

"It's kind of hard to forget," Flynn said. "I didn't even know Jake was gay."

"Pansexual," Logan corrected. "He's attracted to anyone and it doesn't matter about the biological sex or gender identity. And right now, he's attracted to his best friend."

"And why hasn't he told me?" Flynn asked.

"Because he knows he doesn't have a chance with you," Logan said.

"Well, he's right there," Flynn said. "But still. I'm his best friend and I really miss hanging out with him. You know what? I'm going to go talk to him."

"No, don't," Logan said. "He's really going to hate me if he finds out I told you."

"But you didn't," Flynn said. "I was eavesdropping, so he can't get mad at you."

"I told Fin, though," Logan said.

Flynn shrugged. "That's your fault, not mine."

"Flynn, did you hear anything else in the conversation?" I asked.

"No, why?" Flynn asked.

"No reason," I said. I was happy he didn't hear the part about Logan thinking Lilly liked Flynn. There was no way she liked him, and if Flynn heard what Logan said, that would only raise his ego.

Flynn shrugged. "Well, I am going to talk to Jake. And by that, I mean I'm walking over to his house so he can't hide from me."

"Flynn, I really think you should leave it alone," I said.

"No way," Flynn said. "He's my best friend and if he's feeling all sad, I want to be there to comfort him, even if he's sad because of me. When Mom comes home, tell her I'm over at Jake's."

When he left, Logan sighed. "Great. Now Jake is going to be really mad at me."

"I doubt he'll get mad," I said. "He's not really the type of person to get mad."

"I don't know," Logan said. "One time, my dad took Jake's computer away because he pulled an all-nighter on a school night and Jake got really angry. He was swearing and everything."

I snorted. "But that has to do with him not being able to game. I don't think he's going to get mad at you."

"If you say so," Logan said. "So, what do you think the next task is going to be?"

"Who knows?" I said. "I'm pretty sure it will have to do with building the bomb, so we're probably going to have to get something else."

The phone Ryan gave us suddenly beeped, so Logan pulled it out of his pocket and looked at the message. "Well, you're not wrong there," Logan said. "I told you if we talked about it, we would get a message."

"Yeah, whatever," I said. "What does it say?"'

"He's just telling us that we have to get about twenty metal scraps and...." Logan furrowed his eyebrows as he read the message. "We have two new people who will be doing the tasks with us."

"What?" I asked. "Who?"

Logan sighed. "Jake and Lilly."

____

Ooh how fun. cx

Omg, so if you read the message I posted to my followers a few days ago, I was saying how I'm shipping two of my characters, from different series, who are five years apart. One of them is in this series. ;)

AND YOU KNOW WHAT I HATE? Having a large family with only one shower. My sister has been in there for over an hour and a half and she's not even a teenager. She doesn't have to do all this stuff to get ready for bed. -.-

Chapter 17

Whoa, what's this? Two updates in a row?

:D

Chapter 17

I texted Flynn to come back over with Jake as soon as he got to his house. I didn't tell him why, but thankfully Flynn didn't ask. He even said that if Jake refused, he would knock him out with chloroform and drag him over.

For Jake's sake, I really hope he didn't refuse to come over.

I also texted Lilly as well and she showed up within five minutes. "Two questions," she said. "Why am I here? And is Flynn here?"

"Why?" Logan asked before I could say anything. "You miss him?"

Lilly glared at Logan. "No. I just....didn't want to be annoyed by him."

"Uh huh," Logan said. "Fin's too stubborn, but I see right through you."

Lilly snorted. "You really thing I like that annoying, obnoxious boy who is three years younger than me?"

"Yes."

Lilly scoffed and rolled her eyes before sitting on the chair. "You're unbelievable, Fitzgerald."

"Unbelievably true, yes," Logan said.

"Logan, I told you," I said. "She doesn't like him."

"Thank you, Infinity," Lilly said. "At least someone believes me. I don't like Flynn. Maybe I like the attention he gives me, but that's it."

"Uh huh," Logan said with a smile.

"I'm sorry, does this amuse you?" Lilly asked.

"Very much," Logan said. "Flylly will be prevail."

"Shut up," Lilly said.

"What? That's what you said about Loganity before Fin and I got together," Logan said.

"Well, yeah, but that's because you two actually belong together," Lilly said. "Flynn and I don't. Never in a million years. Now can we please change the subject? Why did you want me to come here? Usually, you two would rather be alone so you can make out."

"We don't make out all the time," Logan said. "And just wait for your boyfriend and his best friend to come here."

"He's not my boyfriend," Lilly said. "Infinity, please tell your stupid boyfriend to knock it off."

"Stupid boyfriend, knock it off," I said to Logan.

Logan shrugged, but I knew he wasn't going to leave Lilly alone over this. I highly doubt Lilly liked my brother. I mean, sure, she did ask only Flynn for his opinion on her outfits and sure, she subtly asked for him to flirt with her and sure, whenever we watched a movie together, she always had to sit beside him and....

....Logan was right. I was stubborn.

"So why do we have to wait for Flynn and Jake to come?" Lilly asked.

"We'll tell you when they get here," I said. "But it's not really a good thing."

It didn't take long for Flynn and Jake to show up and as soon as they did, Jake walked over and punched Logan's shoulder. "Okay, one, that didn't hurt at all," Logan said. "And two, why did you punch me."

"For telling Flynn that I liked him," Jake said.

"I did not tell Flynn," Logan said.

"Yes, you did," Flynn said. "You walked up to me and said 'Flynn, Jake has a crush on you'."

I gave Flynn a flat look. "Really? That did not happen."

"Then how did Flynn find out?" Jake asked.

"Because Fin and I were talking about it and he overheard," Logan said, which caused Jake to punch him again.

"You said you weren't going to tell anyone," Jake said.

"Oh, come on, you really think I wasn't going to tell my girlfriend?" Logan asked. "Did you two at least figure things out?"

"Yeah," Jake said. "I'm still mad at you, though."

"Wait," Lilly spoke up. "Jake, you like Flynn?" Jake's reply was to glare at Logan. "And by figure things out, do you mean....dating?"

"Nope," Flynn said. "I don't roll like that. We just talked it out and agreed to stay friends. Besides, I'm kind of taken."

"You are?" Lilly asked. "By who?"

"By a special girl who my heart belongs too," Flynn said. "We're kind of official."

"Are you talking about Lilly?" Logan asked.

"But of course," Flynn said, winking at Lilly.

"I should have guessed that," Lilly muttered. "So. Again. Why are we here?"

"It's about the tasks Logan, Flynn, and I have to do," I said. "We got a message to do another one but this time, you and Jake have to join in."

"Say what now?" Jake asked. "Why? I wasn't even part of it last time."

"I know," Logan said. "We think that Ryan somehow found out that we told you about it, so he's making you two do it now. He told us there would be consequences if we told anyone."

"Well, what's the task?" Flynn asked. "Does it have something to do with the bomb?"

"I think so," Logan said. "We have to get twenty scraps of metal to him within two hours."

"Okay, that's easy enough," Jake said.

"I don't know," Flynn said. "Usually when it seems easy, it's actually really hard."

"No, this one is actually easy," Jake said. "Mike works at a garage and he always has scraps of metal they're selling so we could buy it from there. Easy."

"Not easy," Lilly said. "Don't you have to pay for them?"

"Mike gets a discount if he buys it," Logan said as he took out his phone and sent him a message. Not too long after, he got a message back and he sighed. "He said he would buy it if I do his laundry for a month."

"Sweet, such an easy task," Flynn said. "I don't even have to do anything."

"Are you going to do his laundry for a month?" I asked Logan.

"Why not?" Logan asked. "I'd rather not, but it's a small price to pay to, you know, stay alive."

"Fair point," I said.

Logan replied to Mike. "Okay, he's going to buy it now, so we just have to head over to the garage, then to the drop-off point and we're done this task."

"Yes, then we have to go back to worrying about the gas bomb," Flynn said. "Can't we just tell the cops?"

"No way," Logan said. "Ryan will kill us. Actually kill us."

"And that would kill Mom inside," I told Flynn. "She already lost my dad to Death by Death. She won't be able to handle losing both her children to Death by Death as well."

"Okay, but there has to be something we could do without Ryan finding out," Flynn said. "Hey, Lilly...."

"Don't start," Lilly said.

"I wasn't," Flynn said. "I was going to ask if you remember where their HQ is."

"Actually, I do remember," Lilly said.

"Then we tell the cops where it is and boom, all over," Flynn said.

"Not yet," I said.

"What? Why?" Flynn asked. "Don't you want it to be over?"

"Yes, I do," I said. "But it isn't enough to tell the cops where the HQ is because I bet you anything Ryan isn't hiding out there. He's the dangerous one we have to catch and if the cops go to the HQ and arrest everyone, Ryan will know it was us. We'll think of something but for right now, let's go get the scraps and finish this task.

We left the house and got into Logan's house before he drove to the garage his older brother worked at. When we got there, Logan and I got out to get them and load them into the trunk.

"I still don't get why you need all this metal scrap," Mike said.

"Because there's a robot competition going on at the school and I...." Logan began.

"Boring," Mike interrupted. "Seriously. Stop being a nerd."

"For your information, I like being a nerd," Logan said. "And thank you for buying these for me."

Mike shrugged. "You're doing my laundry. Fair trade. The discount made it not cost as much. Now go be that little nerd you are and build the robot."

"Thanks, Mike," Logan said before he and I got back into the car.

Logan drove to the location of the drop-off and got out of the car to give Ryan the metal scraps. Ryan had a smirk on his face as they talked and he pat Logan's back before walking off with the scraps.

Logan got back into the car. "He said the next one won't be easy," Logan said as he pulled onto the street and began driving back to my house.

"He's always saying that," I said. "I just hope he isn't right about it."

"Do you really think they're going to bu--"

"Can we get McDonald's?" Flynn interrupted.

"And who's going to pay for it?" Logan asked.

"You will, obviously," Flynn said.

"No, I'll pay," Lilly said. "I have my wallet and Logan has to suffer enough from doing Mike's laundry. Did you tell him what the metal scraps were for?"

"No, definitely not," Logan said. "As far as he knows, I'm building a robot for a competition at school. I am never telling Mike or Rebecca about this. I learned my lesson from telling Jake."

"Well, you had to if you wanted me to h--"

"Seriously, I want McDonald's," Flynn said.

"We are getting McDonald's," Logan said. "It takes a while to drive there."

"Then hurry up," Flynn said.

"I'm not speeding," Logan asked. "I don't want to put any of you into any more danger than you're in. I can barely drive as it us because I'm tired from being up most nights resea--"

"McDonald's," Flynn interrupted yet again.

"Are you ever going to let any of us talk?" Logan asked.

"Not until I have chicken nuggets in my mouth," Flynn said.

We shortly got to the McDonald's drive-through with Flynn only inter-rupting us two more times. It took Flynn a while to order what to drink because he was stuck deciding between two different soda flavors so in the end, he got both.

After we got out food, Logan began driving back to my house.

"I wonder if bugs could sink or float," Flynn said as he took the lid off of one of the cups of soda.

"What?" Logan asked.

"I said," Flynn said as he took something off of Logan's shoulder, "I wonder if bugs could sink of float." He then dropped what he was holding into the cup of soda. "Ooh, they sink."

"What was that?" I asked.

"A bug," Flynn said. "Those listening device thingies. Ryan must have planted it on Logan to eavesdrop on us. Not cool."

"So that's why you kept interrupting everyone," I said. "Nice thinking."

"I know, right?" Flynn said. "I really wanted McDonald's though. This was just the perfect opportunity to do so."

Lol, thinking of Jake and Taylor makes me want to finish this book so I can get started on, which will now be, Flynn and Jake's book. I decided to do them both into one book and every chapter would alternate. :D

This book will definitely end before chapter 30. I'm going to get the ending started soon, then have the after-ending, if that makes sense. cx I don't want to say too much so I don't give it away.

Chapter 18

Chapter 18

I was woken up by the doorbell repeatedly ringing over and over again. I sighed and looked at the alarm clock beside my bed. Who would be here at four-thirty in the morning?

I pulled myself out of bed because I figured my mom wasn't going to answer it since she was a heavier sleeper, and she would have already been out of bed by know if she had heard it.

I made my way downstairs and looked through the peephole, seeing Logan standing there. I furrowed my eyebrows and opened the door. "Logan? What are you...."

"We need to get out of here, now," he interrupted.

"What's going on?" I asked.

"I'll explain later, just please, go wake up Flynn," Logan said. "Jake and Lilly are already in the care, but we really need to leave now."

"Okay, okay," I said. "Can you get Flynn? I would rather not be in my pajamas if we're going....wherever it is we're going."

"Sure, but you have to get changed fast," Logan said. He walked in and I closed the door before the two of us headed up the stairs. I went to my room and got changed into the first clothes I grabbed before grabbing my cell phone and my charger before sticking it in the pocket of my hoodie.

As soon as I left my bedroom, Mom walked out of her room. "What's with all the commotion?" she asked. "Why are you up so early?"

"I have no idea, to be honest," I said. "Logan showed up and said Flynn and I have to leave with him now. He doesn't have time to explain what's going on. I'll text you once he tells me, okay?"

"Okay," Mom said. "You'll be okay, right?"

"Yeah," I said, though I didn't really know the answer. I gave her a hug before leaving the house and getting into the passenger seat of the car. I was the last one in so once I was buckled up, Logan pulled out of the driveway and began driving down the road.

"So, can we please know what's going on and why you woke us up so early?" I asked.

Logan sighed. "So, I was up again trying to find anything that will help counter the gas bomb, and my parents must have heard me typing on my laptop, because they came in my room and asked why I was up so late. Well, early. You know what I mean."

"Dad was loud," Jake added. "I heard him from my room. He accused Logan of looking at porn."

I raised an eyebrow. "Were you?"

"No!" Logan said. "I don't do that, and I just told you I was doing research. Anyway, my dad took my laptop and looked at the history and found all these different websites. So I had to come clean because my dad, like always, overreacted and thought I was the one building a bomb. He always jumps to conclusions."

"Okay, I get that you told them, but that doesn't mean we have to leave our homes at four-thirty in the morning," I said.

"Yeah, it does, because my mom called the cops and said Ryan is in town," Logan said. "And, to make things worse, I got a text on my own phone from Ryan, saying that he's coming to get us since the cops are looking for him."

"Well, why didn't you stop your mom?" Flynn asked. "From calling the cops?"

"Uh, have you met my parents?" Logan asked. "They're very stubborn. I tried, Jake was out of bed by then and tried getting her to not call the cops, but she did. So, we're most likely dead."

"Logan, don't think like that," I said.

"I'm only thinking reasonably," Logan said. "He's dangerous, you know that. No doubt he'll kill us because of this, which is why we are leaving town."

I sighed and pulled out my cell phone to text my mom what was happening. "And where will we be going?"

"Uh....What about Canada?"

"Ooh, I'm up for that," Flynn said. "When we get to a hotel, Lilly and I are sharing a room."

"Oh my....How many times do I have to tell you that I don't like you, nor I ever will?" Lilly asked.

"Obviously not enough," Flynn said before winking at Lilly.

Normally, I would have asked Flynn to leave Lilly alone, but now I knew that she actually did like him, so I didn't bother.

I couldn't believe Logan was right the whole time.

More importantly, I couldn't believe one of my best friends liked my younger brother.

"Uh, Logan?" Jake said. "Mind driving a little faster?"

"What? Why?" Logan asked. "I'm driving fast enough."

"Well, yeah, but....I think Ryan is in the car behind us," Jake said.

I looked in the side mirror and I was able to catch a glimpse of Ryan in the driver's seat. "Yeah, he is," I said.

"We're dead," Flynn said. "We're so dead."

"Not yet," Logan muttered before he began driving a bit faster. Since it was almost five in the morning and we lived in such a small town, not too many cars were out so Logan was easily able to get on a highway and drive even faster.

"Where are we going to go?" I asked. "He's following us and we're on the highway and...."

"Fin," Logan interrupted. "I need to concentrate on my driving. Just....trust me."

There was a sudden bang, followed by a loud pop and the car bounced a bit.

"Oh, no," Logan said. "No no no."

"What?" I asked.

"I think h--" Logan was cut off when another set of a bang and a pop followed, this time making the car slow to a bumpy stop. "He shot the tires." Logan tried driving again, but the tires already let out enough air to make it impossible.

Ryan's car pulled up next to ours and he got out. My heart began beating faster at the sight of a gun in his hand. He opened the driver's door. "Get out and into my car and I won't shoot," he said. "And I suggest you do it fast before a single car drives by."

None of us objected as we got out of the car and got into Ryan's. He ordered Logan to sit in the passenger seat and the rest of us had to cram in the back. I sat in the spot behind Logan, hoping that gave him some comfort. I could already see how much it was bothering him as I watched his leg bounce up and down.

"Can I sit in the front?" I asked Ryan before he could even start up the car. "Please?" I couldn't have Logan sit in the passenger seat, not with his anxiety.

"Why?" Ryan asked. "Are you planning something?"

"No, I'm not stupid enough to do that when you have a weapon," I said. "Just....please let Logan sit in the back."

Ryan look at the road, thankfully not seeing a single car in sight. "Fine, but hurry up."

I got out of the car, as did Logan. "Fin, I know you don't want to sit up there."

"I don't, but I can and you can't," I said. "It will be fine as long as we do what he says, okay. Now hurry and get in the backseat."

As soon as Logan and I were back in the car, Ryan started it up and began driving down the highway before taking an exit so we were heading back to town. Why would he take us back there?

It soon made sense when he suddenly pulled into an open field with nothing but a dilapidated shack. He ordered us out of the car and looked at us. "I want all of your cell phones," he said, and none of us hesitated to hand him our cell phones. He then gestured for us to go into the shack and he followed. "Now, I can shoot and kill all of you right here, right now. But I won't."

"Why?" Lilly asked slowly.

"Because I think it would be much more fun for you five to hear about everyone suffering a painful death," he said. "I just need to keep you in here so you don't interfere."

He then left and locked the door behind him. I knew immediately what he was talking about.

"They're building the gas bomb now, aren't they?" Jake asked.

"That's what I'm thinking," I said. "We have to do something."

"We can't," Logan said. "It's over."

"But....there has to be something we can do," I said. "We can't....we can't let all those people die."

"I know," Logan said. "But I don't think there's anything we can do."

Flynn smiled before pulling out his cell phone. "That's where you're wrong," he said.

"Uh....Flynn?" Lilly said. "Why didn't you give Ryan you're cell phone? Once he finds out he only has four and not five...."

"Relax, I'm not an idiot," Flynn said. "Before I left my house, I made sure I grabbed the cell phone Ryan gave us to contact us. That's they one I gave him because it looked identical to mine. I even swapped phone cases just in case. Oh, and I just so happened the remember the license plate number of Ryan's car. So I'm going to tip off to the police that he's going to enter the town soon."

"Flynn, you're amazing!" Lilly said before kissing his cheek.

Flynn was in shock for a bit before he smiled. "I am never washing my cheek again."

Lilly rolled her eyes. She was probably too happy to pretend she didn't like Flynn. "Just shut up and call the police."

———————————————

Ooh, stuff is going to go down next chapter. :D I finally know where this is going, woot woot. Like I said, it will be ending pretty early, but at least the third book will be about both Flynn and Jake. It will alternate their POV's.

Winter Gatherings is making me want to finish this so I can write about the start of Jake and Taylor's relationship. cx

Chapter 19

C hapter 19

"I still think we should try leaving," Jake said. "I don't like being in here."

"We're going to have to wait until we know it's safe," Flynn said. "Besides, how are we going to get back? We'll have to walk it and if Ryan isn't in custody of the police, then we're screwed."

"And how would we know when he's arrested?" Lilly asked.

"Uh, easy," Flynn said. "I have my phone and there's still date. It will be all over the news, so I just check it out. Seriously, you guys need to start thinking more logically and not the simple 'Oh, there's nothing we can do'. Seriously, it's like I'm the only smart person here. Say, Lilly, can you kiss my cheek again for being a genius?"

"No, that was a one time thing," Lilly said.

"You say that now...."

"I'll always be saying that," Flynn said as he took out his phone again, then handing it to Lilly. "Here. Since Ryan is going to get arrested, call the cops and tell them you know the where Death by Death's HQ is."

"Wow, you're really thinking this through," Lilly said. "I'm really tempted to kiss you again." Flynn smiled. "But it's not going to happen."

"Aww...."

Lilly rolled her eyes and called the police, explaining to them who she was and where the HQ is. She also told them where we were and asked if someone could come here to let us out. She then hung up and handed the phone back to Flynn.

"So....Is that kiss still up for grabs?" Flynn asked.

"Not happening."

"No need to be so rude."

"I'm getting bored," Jake whined. "I miss Minecraft."

"We'll play once we wait this out," Flynn said. "Which I'm hoping doesn't take too long."

It felt like hours before we heard a care pull up. Logan went to the small window on the side to check it out. "Oh....No...."

"What?" I asked, walking over as well.

It wasn't the police.

"It's Ryan," Logan said. "And he does not look happy."

"Quick, Flynn, hide your phone," Lilly said.

"What? Why?"

"Because if he finds out you called them, he'll hurt you," Lilly said before grabbing Flynn's cell phone out of the pocket. She didn't have time to hide it because Ryan came it, so she quickly shoved it in her back pocket before he could see.

"Who called the cops?" Ryan asked.

"What are you talking about?" Flynn asked. "You took our cell phones."

"Yeah, I did," Ryan said. "But someone called me and warned me that the cops are waiting by the entry of the town, and they have information about my car, including the license plate."

"So?" Flynn asked. "Someone could have seen you driving with us."

"True, but then I was also told that the cops know the location of the HQ and arrested all but one of the members," he said. "So which one of you called the cops, huh?"

My hand tightened around Logan's arm when I saw Ryan's gun sticking out of his pants' belt. My heart started beating fasted when he reached for the weapon, his hand just resting there.

"Oh, so no one's going to answer?" Ryan said, adjusting his grip on the weapon. His eyes then landed on Flynn. "Was it you? You're always one step ahead of everyone. I wouldn't doubt that you somehow sneaked another phone...." His eyes then narrowed. "The phone I gave you guys for contact. You still have it."

He lifted the gun out of his belt and pointed it at Flynn, but Lilly quickly stood between him. "No, wait! It wasn't him, it was me! I tipped off the police! After all, I'm the only who knows the location of the HQ!"

Ryan narrowed his eyes at her. "I don't believe you."

Lilly reached into her back pocket and pulled out the phone. "The phone is here. I was the only who called them, not Flynn. Do what you want, but please don't hurt him."

"Oh, don't worry, it isn't him I'll be hurting," Ryan said before pulling the trigger, causing a loud Bang to sound and Lilly falling to the ground.

"Lilly!" Flynn said, kneeling down beside her. "Lilly, please be okay...." He quickly took off his sweater and pressed it against the wound on her shoulder.

Logan was going to make sure Lilly was okay, but Ryan turned towards him. "Don't move, any of you," he snapped. "Do you know how hard Death by Death has worked staying out of trouble? Then you come along and suddenly, we're all arrested."

It was their fault, to be honest. If he didn't want this, then they should have chosen another victim, no me and Logan.

However, I was glad they chose us. If they didn't, who knows how long it would take for them to be arrested for their heinous crimes?

"Why?" Logan asked and I could sense a bit of fear behind his voice. "Why do you all have pleasure in killing people?"

"I don't have to answer myself to you," Ryan hissed. "But all five of you are about to pay, starting with...." He pointed the gun at me, but Logan gently pushed me behind him. "Oh, you want to be a hero, don't you? How cute. It's useless. I have plenty of bullets and you have no weapons."

Before he could pull the trigger, the door suddenly burst open with three cops standing there. "Put your weapon down, now!" one yelled.

Ryan didn't do anything. He stayed where he was with his gun pointed at Logan.

"I'm not going to asked again! Weapon down!"

Ryan suddenly turned and fired at one of the cops, and they fired back. I didn't see it. I quickly hid behind Logan, wrapping my arms around his waist and digging my face in his back. My ears began ringing, then suddenly everything was silent.

Logan turned to face me, cupping my face in his hands. "Are you okay?"

I nodded. "Is....Is it over?"

Logan nodded and pulled me into a hug. "It's over, Fin."

One of the police officers stepped outside and called a paramedic over. Once they were inside, they immediately went to Lilly. "Is she going to be okay?" Flynn asked, his voice cracking a bit.

"I would say so, yes," the officer said. "It's a shoulder wound, nothing too bad."

"Yeah, I survived one of those," Flynn said. "Lilly, are you okay?"

"Yeah," she said after a deep breath. "And no, I'm not....I'm not going to kiss you just....in case I don't make it."

Flynn smiled at that. "Well, at least I know you're okay. You totally want me, though."

"That's debatable."

The officer that was shot by Ryan wasn't wounded it all. Ryan ended up hitting his bulletproof vest.

Ryan, on the other hand....

My eyes landed on him laying on the floor. "Is he...."

"Yeah," Logan said. "He is. Come on, let's get some fresh air."

We stepped outside with Jake. Flynn refused to leave Lilly's side.

"Infinity!" I heard someone call. I looked over, seeing Mom stepping out of her car, which was followed by Logan's family getting out of their car, and Lilly's parents.

Mom rushed over and gave me a hug and I hugged her back tightly. "I got a call and I was so worried," she said. "Are you okay? Where's Flynn, is he okay?"

I nodded. "Yeah, we're....we're fine."

"Are you sure?" she asked. "You don't look fine."

"Yeah, I'm just...shaken up," I said. "Lilly got hurt, but she should be fine, and Flynn doesn't want to leave her side."

"That boy is still hopelessly in love with her," Mom said with a chuckle.

"Yeah, but Lilly totally likes him," I said. "I can see it."

"It took you a while to see it," Logan said.

"Oh, shush. I didn't want to believe it."

There were quite a few policemen here, not just the three that went inside. One of them talked to each of our families to see if we were doing okay.

One of the police officers stepped out of the shed and I saw Mom looking at him. "J-Jim?"

He looked over at Mom, smiling faintly. "Jamie."

Logan looked over at me. "Jim?" he mouthed, and I shrugged.

"H-how are you....I mean....You're a-alive," Mom said.

"Yeah," Jim said. "I am. It's a long story."

"Who's this?" I asked Mom.

"Infinity, this is your dad," Mom said and I looked over at him again.

I've seen pictures of my dad. Mom has showed me a lot of them, but they were all from over seventeen years ago. He did age quite a bit, but he looked like the man in all those pictures.

He really was my dad.

And even though I didn't really know him, I rushed over and wrapped my arms around him. He hugged me back tightly. "I am so sorry I wasn't there for you when you were growing up," he said. "But I had to do what I did."

"I would still like an explanation," Mom said.

"Okay, so on the eighth task, the one where I had to drive on the opposite side of the road, I got into a crash and the paramedics got to me first," he explained. "I was still conscious and I explained to them everything, so the police thought it would be best if I faked my death so Death by Death wouldn't kill me for not completing the task. And I couldn't have any contact with you at all, because that would put you in danger. I joined the police to help track and take down Death by Death. I didn't think it would take over seventeen years."

"Infinity?" Flynn suddenly asked, so I looked over at him. "Why are you hugging a police officer?"

"This is my dad," I said.

"Your dad?" Flynn asked. "So....he's alive?"

Dad smiled. "I am. Who are you?"

"I'm Flynn, I'm adopted."

Mom chuckled. "He's my adopted son. I adopted him not too long ago."

"Would this mean you're my dad now?" Flynn asked.

"I think we have to talk about that," Mom said. Dad nodded in agreement, so they walked a bit further away to talk.

"How's Lilly?" I asked Flynn.

"Refusing to kiss me," Flynn said. "It hurts."

"So, she's okay?"

"Yeah, they're taking her to the hospital now to get the bullet out and stitch up the wound," Flynn said. "I'm just glad I didn't lose my future girlfriend. And before you say anything, it will happen. Just you watch."

"I wasn't going to say anything," I said.

"Good," Flynn said. "So....This is all over now."

"Yeah," Logan said. "Only one of the members escaped, but I heard the police are tracking him down right now, and they're going to be officers outside of our homes until his caught. They're not putting us in danger."

"That's....good. It feels weird."

"Yeah, it does," I said. "What about the bomb?"

"What bomb?" Dad asked, now standing beside us again.

"Ooh, that was a fast talk," Flynn said. "Are you two still in love? Please say you are. I don't like living with only females."

Mom smiled. "We are and we're going to have things going back to normal before he was targeted. It's going to be weird, but we're going to make it work."

"Again? What bomb?" Dad asked.

"Oh, they were planning on building this gas bomb," I said. "Hey, Nerd-Pants, what gas were they using again?"

Logan sighed. "Thanks for the nickname. And to answer your question, it's sarin gas."

Dad raised an eyebrow. "That's highly toxic. They were planning on building a bomb with it?" I nodded. "Well, the good news is that I'm guessing that's what they were working on when the police got into the HQ. It wasn't completed, so I'll send a message to the ones still there so they can confiscate the gas."

After he did that, Flynn let out a relieved sigh. "It feels good saving the world."

"What are you talking about?" I asked. "You didn't save the world."

"Uh, I'm sorry, but who was the one that sneaked another cell phone?" he asked. "And called the cops on Ryan? And told Lilly to call the cops to give them the HQ location? Oh, right. Me. I don't care what you said, I saved the world."

———————————————

Flynn totally saved the world, amiright. cx

And you should thank everyone who got me to ship Flynn and Lilly because if I didn't, she would have been dead right now. I was planning on killing her off, but now I can't because Flynn and Lilly for life. cx

There are going to be a few more chapters about them Infinity adjusting to life without Death by Death and with her dad, but the book will be ending soon. Idk how soon, but soon. Maybe chapter 25? I'll probably add a lot of Loganity fluff. cx

Chapter 20 | Final Chapter

The book pretty much ended, so.... Yeah. cx

Chapter 20

"Mom!" Flynn called as we walked into the living room. "I really need some advice. I'm really heartbroken and I think I might cry any second."

"What's wrong?" Mom asked, pausing the movie she was watching with me and Logan.

"I asked a girl out," Flynn said. "And she rejected me."

"Does the girl go by the name of Lilly?" I asked.

"What? No," Flynn said. "Okay, yeah. She will say yes one day, I guarantee it."

I raised an eyebrow. "You really think my best friend is going to have a crush on my little brother?" Even though she totally did.

"Yes," Flynn said. "I mean, who can resist all of this? I already know someone that can't resist me. Starts with a J. Rhymes with ca--"

"Are you always so annoying?" I interrupted. "We're trying to watch a movie."

"Why yes, I am," Flynn said. "There are too many girls in this house. When is Dad coming home?" It didn't really take long for Flynn to start calling my dad 'Dad'. It did feel a bit weird for me at first and it did take me longer than Flynn. I just avoiding trying to get Dad's attention to talk to him so I wouldn't have to call him Dad.

"What do you mean there are too many girls?" Logan asked. "There's Fin and your mom. Then there's me and you. That's two and two."

"Wait, you're a boy?" Flynn asked. "Prove it?"

"I can verify that he is indeed a boy," I said.

Flynn's face scrunched in disgust. "That's disgusting. I didn't need to know that."

"You walked right into that one," I said.

Flynn didn't reply as he huffed and walked into the kitchen, most likely to get food. Mom unpaused the movie and I tried paying attention to it, but it was a bit hard, to be honest. Most of the time, my mind was just occupied thinking about everything I had to go through with Death by Death.

Me thinking I lost one of my two best friends.

Flynn being bitten by a poisonous snake.

Having to rob a bank which resulted in both Logan and Flynn getting shot.

Ryan escaping prison.

Them trying to make a gas bomb.

Seeing Ryan's dead body in the shed....

"You okay?" Logan asked me in a quite voice.

I nodded and released a deep breath. "Yeah. Yeah, it's just....a bit hard getting passed all of what happened. I mean, we're finally free from all of it. All the members are in jail, there's no longer a gas bomb being made, Ryan is....I still can't get passed it."

"Don't worry, you're not the only one," Logan said. "You know me. I tend to hang onto the past longer than I have to."

"Yeah, I know," I said. "It's probably worse on you than it is on me."

"No, don't compare it," Logan said. "It was bad for the both of us. We'll get over it soon, don't worry. It may take a few weeks, months, even years. But at least everything is going well for us. Lilly's alive, your dad's alive."

I gave him a faint smile. "Yeah, that's true. I still can't believe it. For the longest time, it was just me and my mom. Then Flynn came along. And now my dad is actually alive and living with us. Our family is almost perfect."

"Almost?" Logan asked. "What's missing?"

"A dog."

Mom snorted. "You're not getting a dog, Infinity."

"Mom, it's rude to eavesdrop," I said.

"It's kind of hard not to listen in when you're talking over a movie I'm trying to watch," Mom pointed out. "But, all that aside, are you okay?"

"Never better," I said honestly.

The front door opened and Dad walked in, carrying a few bags of takeout food. Flynn immediately ran out of the kitchen. "I smell Chinese food," Flynn said. "Did you bring Chinese food?"

Dad held up the bags. "I did bring Chinese food."

"Yes!" Flynn said happily.

Dad brought the bags to the living room and set them on the table. He noticed Logan sitting there and chuckled. "I see you can't go a single day without coming over," Dad said. "I kind of figured you would be here, so I made sure to get extras."

"Thanks," Logan said.

Once we all got some food and were sitting down, Flynn decided to bring up Lilly yet again. "So, dad, I need advice," Flynn said. "I asked Mom but she's pretty much useless."

"Thanks," Mom said sarcastically.

"What is it?" Dad asked.

"How do you get a girl to like you?" Flynn asked. "I try so hard, but the girl I am in love with doesn't even pay attention to me."

I snorted, but Flynn didn't hear me. Oh, trust me, she did pay attention.

"Does this girl go by the name of Lilly?" Dad asked.

"Yes. She keeps rejecting me and it hurts because I love her so much."

"You're fourteen, Flynn," I said.

"Shut up. She's my soulmate."

"Well, you may hate me for this advice, but you just have to be patient," Dad said. "It may take a while, but maybe she will eventually like you back, maybe she won't. You just have to wait and see."

Flynn huffed. "I can't wait any longer. It hurts me."

"Hey, if it makes you feel better, I had to wait a couple years to start dating Fin," Logan said. "It's really not that bad waiting."

"Whatever."

I rolled my eyes. I did wonder when Lilly wouldn't reject him anymore. Who knows?

9 781787 990982